ENTHRALLED BY MORETTI

BY

CATHY WILLIAMS

MILLS & BOON®

Published in Great Britain 2014
by Mills & Boon, an imprint of Harlequin (UK) Limited,
Eton House, 18-24 Paradise Road, Richmond, Surrey, TW9 1SR

ISBN: 978 0 263 90836 7

Harlequin (UK) Limited's policy is to use papers that are natural, renewable and recyclable products and made from wood grown in sustainable forests. The logging and manufacturing processes conform to the legal environmental regulations of the country of origin.

Printed and bound in Spain
by Blackprint CPI, Barcelona

ENTHRALLED BY MORETTI

To my three wonderful daughters.

CHAPTER ONE

CHASE EVANS PUSHED aside the folder in front of her and glanced at her watch. For the fourth time. She had now been kept waiting in this conference room for twenty-five minutes. As a lawyer, she knew what this was about. Actually, even if she hadn't been a lawyer she would have known what this was about. It was about intimidation. Intimidation by a juggernaut of a company that was determined to get its own way.

She stood up, flexed her muscles and strolled over to the floor-to-ceiling panes of glass that overlooked the teeming streets of the city.

At this time of year, London was swarming with tourists. From way up here, they appeared to be small little stick figures, but she knew if she went down she would join foreigners from every corner of the globe. You couldn't escape them. You couldn't escape the noise, the crowds and the bustle although here, in the opulent surroundings of AM Holdings, you could be forgiven for thinking that you were a million miles away from all that. It was deathly quiet.

Yet another intimidation tactic, she thought cynically. She had seen a lot in the past few years since she had been a practising lawyer, but the antics of this company took some beating.

She thought back to meeting number one, when they

had imagined that buying up the women's shelter would be a walk in the park. For meeting number one, they had sent their junior lawyer, Tom Barry, who had become embroiled in a tangle of logistics with which he had patently been unable to cope.

For meeting number two, they had dispatched a couple of more experienced guys. Alex Cole and Bruce Robins had come prepared, but so had she. Out of all the pro bono cases in which she specialised, the women's shelter was dearest to her heart. If they had come prepared to wipe it out from under her feet, then she too had upped the stakes, pulling out obscure precursors and covenants that had sent them away scratching their heads and promising that they would be back.

Chase had had no doubt that they would. The shelter, or Beth's House, as it was nicknamed, sat on prime land in West London, land that could earn any halfway canny speculator a great deal of money should it be developed. She knew, through contacts and back doors, that it had been targeted for development by the AM group. An ambitious transformation—from a women's shelter to an exclusive, designer shopping mall for the rich and famous.

Well, over her dead body.

Staring down as the minutes of the clock ticked past and no one appeared, she knew that there was a very real possibility that she would have to let this one go, admit defeat. Yet for so many reasons she refused to let herself think that way.

After Alex and Bruce, her next meeting—this time with her boss by her side—had been with their top guy, Leslie Swift. He had cleverly countered every single magic act they had produced from their rapidly shrinking hat. He had produced by-laws, exemptions and clauses that she knew had been designed to have them running back to the drawing board. Now, alone in this sprawling conference room, Chase knew that she was in the last-chance saloon.

Once again she glanced at her watch before moving back to her seat at the thirty-seater table. Lord only knew who they would send this time to take her on. Maybe they would realise that she was mortally wounded and see fit to delegate her right back to the junior lawyer so that he could gloat at the woman who had sent him packing.

But she had one more trick up her sleeve. She wasn't going to give up without a fight. The memory of giving up without fighting was too embedded in her consciousness for her ever to go down that road again. She had dragged herself away from a dark place where any kind of fighting had never been a good idea and she wasn't about to relinquish any of the grit and determination that had got her where she was now.

Banishing all thoughts of a past that would cripple her if she gave it a chance, Chase Evans returned her attention to the file in front of her and the list of names and numbers she had jotted down as her final attempt to win her case.

'Shall I tell Ms Evans how long she might be expected to wait?'

Alessandro Moretti glanced up at his secretary, who stared back at him with gimlet-eyed steeliness. She had announced Chase Evans's arrival half an hour ago, longer, and had already reminded him once that the woman was waiting for him in the conference room. From anyone else, a second reminder would have been unthinkable. Alicia Brown, however, had been with him for five years and it had been clear from the start that tiptoeing around him wasn't going to be on the cards. She was old enough to be his mother and, if she had never tiptoed around any of her five strapping boys, then she certainly wasn't going to tiptoe around anyone. Alessandro Moretti included. He had hired her on the spot.

'You can't keep her waiting for ever. It's rude.'

'But then,' Alessandro countered drily, 'you've been with me long enough to know that I'm rude.' But he stood up and grabbed his jacket from where he had earlier flung it on the long, low, black leather sofa that occupied one side of the office.

In the concrete jungle where fortunes were made and lost on the toss of a coin, and where the clever man knew how to watch his back because the knives were never far away, Alessandro Moretti, at the tender age of thirty-four, ranked as one of the elite pack leaders.

Well, you didn't get to that exalted position by being soft and tender-hearted. Alessandro understood that. He was feared and respected by his employees. He treated them fairly; more than fairly. Indeed they were amongst the highest paid across the board in the city. In return, the line they trod was the line he marked. If he wanted something done, he expected it to be done yesterday. He snapped his fingers and they jumped to immediate attention.

So he was frankly a little put out that his team of lawyers had, so far, singularly failed in nailing the deal with the shelter. He couldn't imagine that it was anything but routine. He had the money to buy them out and so he would. Why then, four months down the line, was he having to step in and do their job for them?

He had elaborate plans to redevelop the extensive land the place was sitting on. His price was more than fair. Any fool should have been able to go in, negotiate and come out with the papers signed, sealed and delivered.

Instead, in a day which was comprised of back-to-back meetings, he was having to waste time with a two-bit pro bono lawyer who had set up camp on the moral high ground somewhere and was refusing to budge. Did he really need to take valuable time out to demolish her? Because demolish her he most certainly would.

He issued a string of orders as he left his office and threw over his shoulder, as he was about to shut the door behind him, 'And don't forget how good I am at sacking people! So I'd better not find that you've forgotten any of what I've just told you! Because I don't see your trusty notepad anywhere…' He grinned and shut the door smartly behind him before his secretary could tell him what she thought of his parting shot.

He was carrying nothing, because as far as he was concerned he didn't need to. He had been briefed on the woman's arguments. He didn't anticipate needing to strong-arm her at all into giving up. He had managed to unearth a couple of covenants barely visible to the naked eye that would subvert any argument she could put forward. Additionally, she had now been waiting for over forty minutes in a conference room that had been deliberately stripped bare of anything that could be seen as homely, comforting, soothing or in any way, shape or form, designed to put someone at ease.

He briefly contemplated summoning those losers who had not been able to do their job so that they could witness first hand how to do it, but decided against it.

One on one. Over and done with in fifteen minutes. Just in time for his next conference call from Hong Kong.

Having had plenty of time to mull over the intimidation tactics, Chase was standing by the window waiting for a team of lawyers. In bare feet, she was five-eleven. In heels, as she was now, she would tower over her opponents. The last one had barely reached her shoulders. Maybe, as a last resort, she could stare them down into submission.

She was gazing out of the window when she heard the

door to the conference room opening behind her and she took her time turning round.

If they could keep her waiting in a room that had all the personality of a prison cell, then she could take her time jumping to attention.

But it wasn't a team of lawyers. It wasn't Tom Barry, Alex Cole, Bruce Robins or Leslie Swift.

She looked at the man standing by the door and she felt the colour drain from her face. She found that she couldn't move from her position of dubious advantage standing by the window. Her legs had turned to lead. Her heart was beating so violently that she felt on the verge of a panic attack. Or, at the very least, an undignified fainting spell.

'You!' This wasn't the strong, steady voice of the self-confident twenty-eight-year-old woman she had finally become.

'Well, well, well…' Alessandro was as shocked as she was but was much more adept at concealing his response and much faster at recovering.

And yet, as he moved slowly towards her, he was finding it almost impossible to believe his eyes.

At the speed of light, he travelled back in time, back to eight years ago, back to the leggy, gloriously beautiful girl who had occupied his every waking hour. She had changed, and yet she hadn't. Gone was the waist-long hair, the jeans and sweater. In its place, the woman standing in front of him, looking as though she had seen a ghost—which he supposed she had—was impeccably groomed. Her shoulder-length bob was the same blend of rich caramel and chestnut, her slanting eyes were as green and feline as he remembered, her body as long and willowy.

'Lyla Evans…' He strolled towards her, one hand in his trouser pocket. 'Should I have clocked the surname? Maybe I would have if it hadn't been preceded by Chase…' He was standing right in front of her now. She looked as though she was about to pass out. He hoped she wouldn't expect him to catch her if she fell.

'Alessandro… No one said… I wasn't expecting…'

'So I see.' His smile was cold and devoid of humour. Of their own accord, his eyes travelled to her finger. No wedding ring. Not that that said very much, all things considered.

'Will you be here on your own, or can I expect the rest of your team…?' Chase tried desperately to regain some of her shattered composure but she couldn't. She was driven to stare at the harsh, sinfully sexy contours of a face that had crept into her head far too many times to count. He was as beautiful as she remembered. More so, if that were possible. At twenty-six, he had been sexy as hell but still with the imprint of youth. Now he was a man, and there was nothing warm or open in his face. She was staring at a stranger, someone who hated her and who was making no attempt to mask his hatred.

'Just me. Cosy, as it turns out. Don't you think? So many years since last we saw one another, Lyla…or Chase, or whoever the hell you really are.'

'Chase. My name is Chase. It always was.'

'So the pseudonym was purely for my benefit. Of course, it makes sense, given the circumstances at the time…'

'Lyla was my mother's name. If you don't mind, I think I'll sit.' She tottered over to the chair and collapsed on it. The stack of files in front of her, her briefcase, her laptop, they were all reminders of why she was in this conference room in the first place, but for the life of her she couldn't focus on them. Her thoughts were all over the place.

'So, shall we play a little catch-up, Lyla? Sorry…Chase? A little polite conversation about what we've been doing for the past eight years?' Alessandro perched on the edge of the sprawling conference table and stared down at her:

the one and only woman he had wasted time chasing, only to be left frustrated when she'd failed to fall into his bed. For that reason alone, she occupied a unique spot in his life. Add all the other reasons and she was in a league of her own.

'I'd rather not.'

'I bet. In your shoes, I'd plead the fifth as well.'

'Alessandro, I know what you must think of me, but—'

'I really don't need to hear any sob stories, Lyla.'

'Stop calling me that. My name is Chase.'

'So you became a lawyer after all. I take my hat off to you—although, thinking about it, you did prove you were the sort of girl who would get what she wanted whatever the cost…'

Chase's eyes flickered up to him. The expression on his face sent the chill of fear racing up and down her spine, yet how could she blame him? Their story had been brief and so full of things that had to be hidden that it was hardly surprising.

'And I notice that there's no telling wedding ring on your finger,' he continued in the same mildly speculative voice that wouldn't have fooled an idiot. 'Did you dispose of the hapless husband in your ever-onwards and upwards climb?'

When he had met her—sitting there in the university canteen with a book in front of her, a little frown on her face, completely oblivious to everyone around her—she had knocked him sideways. It was more than the fact that she'd stood out, that she possessed head-turning looks; the world was full of girls who could turn heads. No, it had been her complete and utter indifference to the glances angled in her direction. He had watched as she had toyed with her sandwich before shoving it to one side and heading out. She had looked neither right nor left. The canteen could have been devoid of people.

Standing here now, looking at her, Alessandro could recreate that feeling of intense, incomprehensible attraction that had swept over him then as though it had been yesterday.

Significantly, she hadn't been wearing a wedding ring then either.

'I'm not here to talk about my past,' Chase said, clearing her throat. 'I've brought all the paperwork about the shelter.'

'And I'm not ready to talk about that yet.' He sat on one of the chairs alongside her and angled it away from the table so that he had a bird's eye view of her as she stared down at the bundle of files and papers in front of her and pretended to concentrate. 'So…' he drawled. 'You were about to tell me where the wedding ring's gone…'

'I don't believe I was,' Chase said coolly, gathering herself. Eyes the colour of bitter chocolate bored straight through her, bypassing the hard, glossy veneer she had taken so much time and trouble to build like a fortress around herself. 'You might be curious about what I've been up to for the past few years, Alessandro, but I have no intention of satisfying your curiosity. I just want to do what I came here to do and leave.'

'You came here to lose to me,' Alessandro told her without preamble. 'If you had any sense, you would recognise that and wave the white flag before I start lowering the price I've offered to pay for that place.' He drew her attention to the clock on the wall. 'With every passing minute, I drop my price by a grand, so make sure your argument's a winning one, because if it's not you're going to find that you're not working on behalf of your client.'

'You can't do that.'

'I can do whatever I like, Lyla…Chase…or shall I call you Mrs Evans? Or perhaps *Ms*...?'

'This isn't about *us,* Alessandro.' She tried to claw the

conversation back to the matter at hand, back to the shelter. 'So please don't think that you can use empty threats to—'

'Look around you,' Alessandro cut in lazily. 'And tell me what you see.'

'Where are you going with this?'

'Just do as I ask.'

Chase looked around nervously. She could feel the jaws of a trap yawning around her, but when she tried to figure out what sort of trap she came up empty. 'Big, bland conference room,' she told him in a voice that hinted that she was already bored with the subject. When she looked around her, her eyes kept wanting to return to him, to look at his face and absorb all the small changes there. Seeing him now, she was beginning to realise that she had never entirely forgotten him. She had buried him but it had obviously been in a shallow grave.

'I like it bland. It doesn't pay to provide distractions when you want the people seated at this table to be focused.'

'*You* like it bland...'

'Correct. You see, I am AM Holdings. I own it all. Every single deal is passed by me. What I say goes and no one contradicts me. So, when I tell you that I intend to drop my price by a grand for every minute you argue with me, I mean it and it's within my power to do it. Of course, you're all business and you think you can win, in which case my threat will be immaterial. But if you don't, well, after a couple of hours of futile arguing... Do the maths.'

Chase looked at him, lost for words. In view of what had happened between them, the deceit and the half-lies that had finally been her undoing, she was staring at a man who had been gifted his revenge. She should have done her homework on the company more thoroughly, but she had been handed the case after her boss had done the preliminaries himself, only to find that he couldn't follow through for personal reasons. She had focused all her energies on trying to locate loopholes that would prevent the sale of the shelter to *anyone* rather than specifically to AM Holdings. Even so, would she have recognised Alessandro had his name cropped up? They hadn't afforded much time for surnames.

'Sounds ungentlemanly.' Alessandro gave an elegant shrug and a smile that was as cold as the frozen wastelands. 'But, when it comes to business, I've always found that being a gentleman doesn't usually pay dividends.'

'Why are you doing this? How could you think of punishing those helpless women who use the shelter because we…we…?'

'Had an ill-fated relationship? Because you lied to me? Deceived me? Does your firm of lawyers know the kind of person you really are?'

Chase didn't say anything but she could feel her nervous system go into overdrive. She had inadvertently stepped into the lion's den; how far did revenge go? What paths would it travel down before it was finally satisfied? Alessandro Moretti owned this place. Not only was it within his power to do exactly as he said, to reduce the amount he was willing to pay for the shelter with each passing minute, but what if he decided actively to go after *her*?

'Things weren't what they seemed back then, Alessandro.'

'The clock's ticking.' He relaxed and folded his hands behind his head. Against all odds, and knowing her for what she really was, he was irritated to discover that he could still appreciate her on a purely physical level. He had never laid a finger on her but, hell, he had fantasised about it until his head had spun, had wondered what she would look like underneath the student clothes, what she would feel like. By the time he had met her, he had already bedded his fair share of women, yet she had appealed to him on a level he had barely comprehended.

He hadn't gone to the university intending to get involved with anyone. He had gone there as a favour to his old don, to give a series of business lectures, to get students inspired enough to know that they could attempt to achieve in record time what he had succeeded in achieving. Six lectures charting business trends, showing how you could buck them and still come out a winner, and he would be gone. He hadn't anticipated meeting Lyla—or, as she now called herself, Chase—and staying on to give a further six lectures.

For the first time in his very privileged life, he had found himself in a situation with a woman over which he'd had little control and he had been prepared to kick back and enjoy it. For someone to whom things had always come easy, he had even enjoyed the hard-to-get game she had played. Of course, he had not expected that the hard-to-get game would, in fact, lead nowhere in the end, but then how was he to know the woman he had been dealing with? She had left him with the ugly taste of disillusionment in his mouth and now here she was…

Wasn't fate a thing of beauty?

'You're not interested in reliving our…exciting past. So, sell me your arguments… And, by the way, that's one minute gone…'

Feeling that she had stepped into a nightmare, Chase opened the top file with trembling fingers. Of course she could understand that he was bitter and angry with her. And yet in her mind, when she had projected into a future that involved her accidentally running into him somewhere, his bitterness and anger had never been so deep, nor had he been vengeful. He could really hurt her, really undo all the work she had done to get where she had.

She began going over some of the old ground covered

in the past three meetings she'd had with his underlings, and he inclined his head to one side with every semblance of listening, before interrupting her with a single slash of his hand.

'You know, of course, that none of those obstructions hold water. You're prevaricating and it won't work.'

Chase involuntarily glanced at the clock on the wall and was incensed that the meeting—all the important things that had to be discussed, things that involved the lives of other people—had been sidelined by this unfortunate, unexpected and worrying collision with her past.

And yet she lowered her eyes and took in the taut pull of expensive trousers over his long legs, the fine, dark hair that liberally sprinkled his forearms… Not even the unspoken atmosphere of threat in his cool, dark eyes could detract from the chiselled perfection of his face. He had the burnished colour of someone of exotic blood.

When she had first laid eyes on him, she had been knocked sideways. He hadn't beaten about the bush. He had noticed her, he said, had seen her sitting in the university canteen. She had instinctively known that he had been waiting for a predictable response. The response of a woman in the presence of a man who could have whoever he wanted, and he wanted her. She had also known that there was no way she could go there. That she should smile politely and walk away, because doing anything else would have been playing with fire. But still she had hesitated, long enough for him to recognise a mutual interest. Of course, it had always been destined to end badly, but she hadn't been able to help herself.

She tightened her lips as she realised just how badly things could go now, all these years later.

'Okay, so you may have all the legalities in place, but what do you think the press would make of a big, bad company rolling in and bulldozing a women's shelter? The public has had enough of powerful people and powerful companies thinking that they can do exactly as they like.' This had been her trump card but there was no hint of triumph in her voice as she pulled it out of the bag.

'I have names here,' she continued in the gathering silence, not daring to risk a glance at him. 'Contacts with journalists and reporters who would be sympathetic to my cause…' She shoved the paper across to him and Alessandro ignored it.

'Are you threatening me?' he asked in a tone of mild curiosity.

'I wouldn't call it threatening…'

'No? Then what exactly *would* you call it?'

'I'm exercising leverage.' It had seemed an excellent idea at the time, but then she hadn't banked on finding herself floundering in a situation she couldn't have envisaged in a million years. His dark eyes focused on her face made her want to squirm and she knew that her veneer of self-confidence and complete composure was badly undermined by the slow tide of pink colour rising to her face. 'If you buy the shelter in a cloud of bad publicity, whatever you put up there will be destined to fail. It's quite a small community in that particular part of London. People will take sides and none of them will be on yours.'

'I bet you thought that you'd bring that out from up your sleeve and my lawyers would scatter, because there *is* such a thing as bad publicity being worse than no publicity. It's a low trick, but then I'm not surprised that you would resort to low tricks.' He leaned forward, rested both arms on the shiny conference table and stared directly at her. 'However, let's just turn that threat on its head for a minute…'

'It's not a threat.'

'I have offered an extremely generous price for the purchase of the shelter and the land that goes with it. More than enough for another shelter to be built somewhere else.'

'They don't *want* to build another shelter somewhere else. These women are accustomed to Beth's House. They feel safe there.'

'*You* can wax lyrical to your buddies at the press that they're being shoved out unceremoniously from their comfort zone. My people will counter-attack with a long, detailed and extremely enticing list of what they could buy for the money they'll be getting from me. A shelter twice the size. All mod cons. An equal amount of land, albeit further out. Hell, they could even run to a swimming pool, a games room, a nursery...the list goes on.

'So, who do you think will end up winning the argument? And, when it comes to light that I will be using the land for a mall that will provide much-needed jobs for the locals, well, you can see where I'm going with this...' He stood up and strolled lazily towards the very same window through which she had been peering earlier.

Chase couldn't tear her eyes away from him. Like an addict in the sudden presence of her drug of choice, she found that she was responding in ways that were dangerously off-limits. She shouldn't be reacting like this. She couldn't afford to let him into her life, nor could she afford to have any deep and meaningful conversations about their brief and ruined past relationship. Heck, it had only lasted a handful of months! And had never got off the starting block anyway.

'So.' Alessandro turned slowly to face her. With his back to the window, the light poured in from behind, throwing his face into shadows. 'How are you feeling about your ability to win this one now?'

'It's Beth's place; she's comfortable there. Why do you think people fight to stay in their homes when a developer comes along promising to buy them out for double what their place is worth?' But he would be able to sell it across the board. He had the money and the people to make sure that whatever message they wanted to get across would be successful. She knew Beth. Was she fighting to preserve something for reasons that were personal?

'I can tell from your expression that you already know that you're staring defeat in the face. By the way, it's been nearly forty-five minutes of unconvincing arguing from you… So how much have you lost your client already? The games room? The nursery? The giant kitchen with the cosy wooden table where all those women can hold hands and break bread?'

'I never thought that you were as arrogant as I now see you are.'

'But then you could say that we barely knew anything about each other. Although, in fairness, I didn't lie about my identity…' He was unconsciously drawn to the way the sunlight streaming through the panes of glass caught the colours of her hair. Her suit was snappy and business-like and he could tell that it had been chosen to downplay her figure. In his mind's eye, he saw the tight jeans, the jumpers and trainers, and that tentative smile that had won him over.

Chase stared down at the folder in front of her. There was nothing left to pull out of the hat. Even if there was, this was personal. He was determined to win the final argument, to have the last word, to *make her pay.*

'So I'm guessing from your prolonged silence that you'll be breaking the happy news to… What's her name? Beth?'

'You know it is.'

'And can you work out how much I'll be deducting from my initial offer?'

'Tell me you don't really mean to go through with that?'

'Lie, in other words?' Alessandro walked towards her and perched on the edge of the table.

'You can't force them to sell.'

'Have you had a look at their books? They're in debt.

Waiting to be picked off. It may be a caring, sharing place, but what it gains in the holding hands and chanting stakes it lacks in the accountancy arena. A quiet word in the right banker's ear and they'll be facing foreclosure by dusk. Furthermore, if it becomes widespread knowledge that they're in financial trouble, the vulture developers will swoop in looking for a bargain. What started out as a generous offer from me would devolve into an untidy fire sale with the property and land going for a song.'

'Okay.' Chase recognised the truth behind what he was saying. How could this be the same man who had once teased her, entertained her with his wit, impressed her with the breadth of his intelligence…driven her crazy with a longing that had never had a chance to be sated?

'Okay?'

'You win, Alessandro.' She looked at him with green eyes that had once mesmerised him right out of the rigidly controlled box into which he had always been accustomed to piling his emotional entanglements with the opposite sex. 'But maybe you could tell me whether you would have been as hardline if I hadn't been the person sitting here trying to talk you out of buying the shelter.'

'Oh, the sale most certainly would have gone ahead,' Alessandro drawled without an ounce of sympathy. 'But I probably wouldn't have tacked on the ticking clock.'

He strolled round to his chair and sat back down. His mobile phone buzzed, and when his secretary told him to get a move on because she could only defer his conference call for so long he informed her briefly that she would have to cancel it altogether. 'And make sure the same goes for my meetings after lunch,' he murmured, not once taking his eyes off Chase's downbent head. He signed off just as Alicia began to launch into a curious demand to know why.

'I don't want to keep you.' Chase began stacking all her files together and shoving them into her capacious brief case. She paused to look at him. *Last look*, she thought. *Then I'll never see you again.* She found that she was drinking in his image and she knew, with resignation, that what she looked at now would haunt her in the weeks to come. It was just so unfair. 'But I would like it if you could reconsider your…your…'

'Lower offer? And save you the humiliation of having to tell your client that you single-handedly knocked the price down?'

Chase glared at him. 'I never took you for a bully.'

'Life, as we both know, is full of cruel shocks. I'll admit that I have no intention of pulling out of this purchase, but you could recoup the lost thousands.'

'Could I? How?' She stared at him. At this point, the images of those wonderful additions to any other house Beth might buy vanishing in a puff of smoke, because of her, were proliferating in her head, making her giddy. She knew that the finances for the shelter were in serious disarray. They would need all the money they could get just to pay off the debts and wipe the slate clean.

'We have an unfinished past,' Alessandro murmured. 'It's time to finish it. I wouldn't have sought out this opportunity but, now it's here, I want to know who the hell you really are. Satisfy my curiosity and the full price is back on the table…'

CHAPTER TWO

SO WHERE WAS the jump for joy, the high five, the shriek of delight? For the sake of a little conversation, she stood to claw back a substantial amount of money. He might have expected some show of emotion, even if only in passing.

Alessandro didn't take his eyes off her face, nor did he utter a word; the power of silence was a wonderful thing. Plus, he didn't trust her as far as he could throw her. If she thought that she could somehow screw him for more than the agreed amount, then let her have all the silence in the world, during which she could rethink any such stupid notion.

'I would need any assurances from you in writing,' Chase finally said. He wanted to finish business between them? Didn't he know that that was impossible? There were no questions she could ever answer and no explanations she could ever give.

'You will be getting no such thing,' Alessandro assured her calmly. 'You take my word for it or you leave here with your wallet several shades lighter.'

'There's no point rehashing what happened between us, Alessandro.'

'Your answer: yes or no. Simple choice.'

Chase stood up and smoothed down her grey skirt. She knew that she had a good figure, very tall and very slender. It was a bonus because it meant that she could pull off cheap clothing; she felt she needed simply to blend in with the other lawyers and paralegals in the company where she worked. Fitzsimmons was a top-ranking law firm and it employed top-ranking people; no riff-raff. Nearly everyone there came from a background where Mummy and Daddy owned second homes in the country. She kept her distance from all of them, but still she knew where they came from just by listening to their exploits at the weekends, the holidays they booked and the Chelsea apartments they lived in.

Thankfully, she was one of only two specialising in pro bono cases, so she could keep her head down, put in her hours and attend only the most essential of social functions.

She didn't want her quiet life vandalised. She didn't want Alessandro Moretti strolling back into it, asking questions and nursing a vendetta against her. She just couldn't afford to have any cans of worms opened up.

Likewise, she didn't want to feel this scary surge of emotion that made her go weak at the knees. Her life was her own now, under control, and she didn't want to jeopardise that.

But where were the choices? Did she make Beth pay for what *she* didn't want? Did she risk her boss's disapproval when she turned up and recounted what had happened?

More than that, if she kept her lips tightly buttoned up, who was to say that Alessandro would conveniently disappear? The way those hard, black eyes were watching her now…

She sat back down. 'Okay. What do you want to talk about? I mean, what do you want me to say?'

'Now, you don't really expect us to have a cosy little chat in a room like this, do you?'

He began prowling around the conference room: thick cream carpet aided and abetted the silence; cream walls;

the imposing hard-edged table where the great and the good could sit in front of their opened laptops, conversing in computer-speak and making far-reaching decisions that could affect the livelihoods of numerous people lower down the food chain, often for the better, occasionally for the worst.

'I mean, we have so much catching up to do, Lyla… Chase…'

'Please stop calling me Lyla. I told you, I don't use that name any more.'

'It's approaching lunchtime. Why don't we continue this conversation somewhere a little more comfortable?'

'I'm fine here.'

'Actually, you don't have a vote. I have five minutes' worth of business to deal with. I trust you can find your way down to the foyer? And don't…' he positioned himself neatly in front of her '…even think of running out on me.'

'I wouldn't do that.' Chase tilted her chin and stood up to look him squarely in the eyes. As a show of strength, it spectacularly backfired because, up close and personal like this, she could feel all her energy drain out of her, leaving behind a residue of tumultuous emotions and a dangerous, scary *awareness.* Her nostrils flared as she breathed in the clean, woody, aggressively masculine scent of his cologne. She took an unsteady step back and prayed that he hadn't noticed her momentary weakness.

'No?' Alessandro drawled, narrowing his eyes. 'Because right now you look like a rabbit caught in the headlights. Why? It's not as though I don't already know you for a liar, a cheat and a slut.' He had never addressed a woman so harshly in his life before but, looking at her here, taking in the perfection of a face that could launch a thousand ships and a body that was slender but with curves in all the right places, the reality of their past had slammed into him and lent an ugly bitterness to every word that passed his lips.

'I notice you're not defending yourself,' he murmured. He didn't know whether her lack of fight was satisfying or not. Certainly, he wished that she would look at him when he spoke, and he was sorely tempted to angle her face to him.

'What's the point?' Chase asked tightly. 'I'll meet you in the foyer but…' she looked at him with a spurt of angry rebellion '…I won't be hanging around for an hour while you take your time seeing to last-minute business with your secretary.'

Alessandro's eyes drifted down to her full, perfectly shaped mouth. He used to tease her that she looked as though she was sulking when it was in repose, but when she smiled it was like watching a flower bloom. He had never been able to get his fill of it. She certainly wasn't smiling now.

'Actually, you'll hang around for as long as I want you to.'

'Just because you want to…to…pay me back for…'

'Like I said, let's save the cosy chit-chat for somewhere more comfortable.'

Only when he left the room did Chase realise how tense she had been. She sagged and closed her eyes, steadying herself against the table.

She felt like the victim of a runaway truck. In a heartbeat, her life seemed to have been derailed, and she had to tell herself that it wasn't so; that because Alessandro was the man with whom she was now having to deal, because their paths had crossed in such a shadowy manner, it didn't mean that he was out to destroy her. His pride had been injured all those years ago and what he wanted from her now was answers to the questions he must have asked himself in the aftermath of their break-up. Not that they had ever really had a *relationship.*

Of course, she would have to be careful with what she told him, but once he was satisfied they would both return to their lives and it would be as if they had never met again.

She left the conference room in a hurry. It was almost twelve-thirty and there were far more people walking around than when she had first entered the impressive building. Workers were going out to lunch. It was a perfect summer's day. There would be sandwiches in the park and an hour's worth of relaxing in the sun before everyone stuck back on their jackets and returned to their city desks. Chase had always made sure to steer clear of that.

In the foyer, she didn't have long to wait before she spotted Alessandro stepping out of the lift. As he walked towards her, one finger holding the jacket that he had tossed over his shoulder, she relived those heady times when she had enjoyed kidding herself that her life could really change. Every single time she had seen him, she had felt a rush of pure, adrenaline-charged excitement, even though all they ever did was have lunch together or a cappuccino somewhere.

'So you're here.'

'You didn't really expect me to run away?' Chase fell into step alongside him. It was a treat not to tower over a guy but she still had to walk quickly to match his pace as they went through the revolving glass doors and out into the busy street.

'No, of course I didn't. You're a lawyer. You know when diplomacy is called for.' He swung left and began walking away from the busier streets, down the little side roads that gave London such character. 'And, on the subject of your career, why don't we kick off our catch-up with that?'

'What do you want to know?'

Alessandro leaned down towards her. 'Let's really get

into the spirit of this, Chase. Let's not do a question-and-answer session, with me having to drag conversation out of you.'

'What do you expect, Alessandro? I don't want to be here!'

'I'm sure you don't, but you're here now, so humour me.'

'I…I…got a first-class degree. In my final year I was head-hunted by a firm of lawyers—not the ones I work for now, but a good firm. I was fast-tracked.'

'Clever Chase.'

Chase recognised that it hadn't been said as a compliment, although she could only guess at what he was implying. He loathed her so, whatever it was, she had no doubt that it would be offensive.

Yet, she *was* clever. In another place and another time, she knew that she would have been one of those girls who would have been said to 'have it all': brains and looks. But then, life had a way of counter-balancing things. At any rate, she had relied far more on her brains than she ever had on her looks. She had worked like a demon to get her A-levels, fought against all odds to get to a top university, and once there had doggedly spared no effort in getting a degree that would set her up for life. And all that against a backdrop that she had trained herself never to think about.

'Thank you.' She chose to misinterpret the tone of his voice. 'So, I got a good job, did my training, changed companies…and here I am now.'

'Fitzsimmons. Classy firm.'

'Yes, it is.' She could feel fine prickles of nervousness beading her forehead.

'And yet, no designer suit? Don't they pay you enough?'

Chase cringed with embarrassment. He had never made any secret about the fact that he came from money. Was that how he could spot the fact that her clothes were off the peg and ready to wear from a chain store? 'They pay me more than enough,' she said coolly. 'But I prefer to save my money instead of throwing it away to a high-end retailer.'

'How noble. Not a trait I would tend to associate with you.'

'Can't you at least try and be civil towards me?' Chase asked thinly. 'At any rate, most of my work is pro bono. It's sensible not to show up in designer suits that cost thousands.' It was what she had laughingly told someone at the firm ages ago and her boss had applauded her good sense.

They were now in front of an old-fashioned pub nestled in one of the quieter back alleys. There were gems like this all over London. When they entered, it was dark, cool and quiet. He offered her a drink and shrugged when she told him that she would stick to fruit juice.

'So…' Alessandro sat down, hand curved round his pint, and looked at her. He honestly didn't know what he hoped to gain from this forced meeting but seeing her again had reawakened the nasty questions she had left unanswered. 'Let's start at the beginning. Or maybe we should pick it up at the end—at the point when you told me that you were married. Yes, maybe that's the place we should start. After we'd been meeting for four months… Four months of flirting and you gazing at me all convincingly doe-eyed and breathless, then informing me that you had a husband waiting in the wings.'

Chase nursed her fruit juice. She licked her lips nervously. Her green eyes tangled and clashed with cold eyes the colour of jet. 'I don't see what the point of this is, Alessandro.'

'You know what the point of it is—you're going to satisfy my curiosity in return for the full agreed price for your shelter. It's a fair exchange. Tell me what happened to the husband.'

'Shaun…was killed shortly after I got my first job. He… he was on his motorbike at the time. He was speeding, lost control, crashed into the central reservation on the motorway…'

'So you didn't ditch him in the impersonal confines of a divorce court.' Nor would she have. Alessandro downed a mouthful of beer and watched her over the rim of the glass. Not, as she had told him on that last day in exhaustive detail, when he'd been her childhood sweetheart and the love of her life. 'And I take it you never remarried.'

'Nor will I ever.' She could detect the bitterness that had crept into her voice, but when she looked at him his expression was still as cool and unrelenting as it had been.

'Is that because there's no room for a man in the life of an ambitious, high-flying lawyer? Or because you're still wrapped up with the man who was…let me try and remember… Oh, yes, I've got it: the only guy you would ever contemplate sleeping with. *Sorry if you got the wrong idea, Alessandro. A few cappuccinos does not a relationship make, but it's been a laugh...*'

'We should never have seen each other. It was a terrible idea. I never meant to get involved with anyone.'

'But you didn't get involved with me, did you?' Alessandro angled his beautiful head to one side as he picked up an unspoken message he wasn't quite getting.

What was there to get or not get? he thought impatiently. The woman had strung him along, led him up the garden path and then had casually disappeared without a backward glance. Hell, she had made him feel things… No, he wasn't going to go there.

'No! No, I didn't. I meant…'

'I'm all ears.'

'You don't understand. I shouldn't even have even to you. I was married.'

'So why did you? Were you riding high on the knowledge that you'd managed to net the rich guy all the groupie students were after?'

'That's a very conceited thing to say.'

'I value honesty. I lost track of the number of notes I got from girls asking for some "extra tuition".'

If there hadn't been notes, she thought, then he surely would have clocked the stares he'd garnered everywhere he went. The man was an alpha male with enough sex appeal to sink a ship. Throw in his wealth, and it was little wonder that girls were queuing up to see if they could attract his attention. She'd never, ever been at the university longer than was strictly necessary but, if she had been, she knew that she would have become a source of envy, curiosity and dislike.

'So was that why you decided to keep your marital status under wraps? To take the wedding ring off? To string me along with the promise of sex?'

'I never said we would end up in bed.'

'Do me a favour!' He slammed his empty glass on the table and Chase jumped. 'You knew exactly what you were getting into!'

'And I didn't think… I never thought…'

'So you lied about the fact that you weren't single or available for a relationship.'

'If I remember correctly, you once told me that you weren't interested in commitment, that you liked your relationships fast and furious and temporary!'

Alessandro flushed darkly. 'Weak reasoning,' he gritted cuttingly. 'Did you lie because you thought that you might try me out for size? See whether I wasn't a better bet than the stay-at-home husband? Is that why you strung me along for four months? Were you hedging your bets?' He shook his head, furious with himself for losing control of the conversation, for actually caring one way or another what had or hadn't been done eight years previously.

'No, of course not! And Shaun was never a *stay-at-*

home husband.' Again, that bitterness had crept into her voice.

'No? So what was he, then?' Alessandro leaned forward, the simple shift of body weight implying threat. 'Banker? Entrepreneur? If I recall, you were a little light on detail. In fact, if my memory serves me right, you couldn't wait to get out of my company fast enough the very last time we met.'

Alessandro was surprised to find that he could remember exactly what she had been wearing the very last time he'd laid eyes on her: a pair of faded skinny jeans tucked into some cheap imitation-suede boots and a jumper which now, thinking about it, had probably belonged to the 'childhood sweetheart' husband. On that thought, his jaw clenched and his eyes darkened.

It hadn't taken her long to spill out the truth. Having spent months of innocent conversation, tentative advances and retreats and absolutely no physical contact—which had been hell for him—she had sat down opposite him at the wine bar which had become their favourite meeting place; at a good bus ride away, it was far from all things university. With very little preamble, and keeping her eyes glued to his face while around them little clusters of strangers had drunk, laughed and chatted, all very relaxed in the run-up to Christmas, she'd informed him that she would no longer be seeing him.

'Sorry,' he recalled her saying with a brittle smile. 'It's been a laugh, and thanks for all the help with the economics side of the course, but actually I'm married…'

She had wagged her ring finger in front of him, complete with never-before-seen wedding band.

Shaun McGregor, she had said airily. Love of her life. Had known him since they were both fifteen. She had even pulled out a picture of him from her beaten-up old wallet and waxed lyrical about his striking good looks.

Alessandro had stared long and hard at the photo of a young man with bright blue eyes and a shaved head. There was a tattoo at the side of his neck; he'd probably been riddled with them. It had been brought home to him sharply just what a fool he had been taken for. Not only had she strung him along for fun, but he had never actually been her type. Her husband had had all the fine qualities of a first-rate thug.

'Shaun did lots of different things,' Chase said vaguely. 'But none of that matters now, anyway. The fact is, I'm sorry. I know it's late in the day to apologise, but I'm apologising.'

'Why did you use a different name?'

'Huh?'

'You used the name Lyla. Not just with me, with everyone. Why?'

'I...' How could she possibly explain that she had been a different person then? That she had had the chance to create a wonderful, shiny new persona, and that she had taken it, because what she could create had been so much better than the reality. She had still been clever, and she had never lied about her academic history but, she had thought, what was the harm in passing herself off as just someone normal? Someone with a solid middle-class background and parents who cared about her? It hadn't been as though she would ever have been required to present these mysterious and fictitious parents to anyone.

And she had always made sure never to get too close to anyone—until Alessandro had come along. Even then, at the beginning, she had had no idea that she would fall so far, so fast and so deep, nor that the little white lies she had told at the beginning would develop into harmful untruths that she'd no longer be able to retract.

'Well?' Alessandro prompted harshly. 'You lied about your single status and you lied about your name. So let's take them one at a time.' He signalled to a waitress and ordered himself another glass of beer. There went the afternoon, was the thought that passed through his mind. There was little chance he would be in the mood for a series of intense meetings and conference calls later. He was riveted by the hint of changing expressions on her face. He felt that he was in possession of a book, the meaning of which escaped him even though he had read the story from beginning to end. Then he cursed himself for being fanciful, which was so unlike him.

'Lyla was my mother's name. I like it. I didn't think there was anything wrong in using it.'

'And so you stopped liking it when you decided to join a law firm?'

'You said we weren't going to do a question-and-answer session!' Her skin burned from the intensity of his eyes on her. Alessandro Moretti, even as a young man in his mid-twenties, had always had a powerful, predatory appeal. There was something dangerous about him that sent shivers up and down her spine and drew her to him, even when common sense told her it was mad. He certainly hadn't lost that appeal.

'It was easier to just use my real name when I joined Edge Ellison, that first law firm. I mean, my Christian name.'

'Why am I getting the feeling that there are a thousand holes in whatever fairy story you're spinning me?'

'I'm not spinning you a fairy story!' Chase snapped. Bright spots of colour stained her cheeks. 'If you want, I can bring my birth certificate to show you!' Except that would suggest a second meeting, which was not something that was going to be on the cards.

But what would he do if he found out where she really came from? What would he do if he discovered that the solid, middle-class background she had innocently hinted at had been about as real as a swimming pool in the middle of the Sahara?

He might be tempted to have a quiet chat with the head of her law firm, she thought with a sickening jolt. Of course, she hadn't lied about any of her qualifications, and she knew that she was a damned good lawyer. There was no way she could be given the sack for just allowing people to *assume* a background that wasn't entirely true, yet…

Wounded pride and dislike could make a person do anything in their power to get revenge. What if he shared all her little white lies with the people she worked with—the posh, private-school educated young men and women who weren't half as good as she was but who would have a field day braying with laughter at her expense? She was strong, but she knew that she was not so strong that she could survive ridicule at the work place.

'I should be getting back to work.' She drained the remainder of her orange juice and made to stand up.

Without thinking, Alessandro reached out and circled his hand around her wrist.

Chase froze. Really, it was the most peculiar sensation…as if her entire body had locked into place so that she was incapable of movement. His fingers around her wrist were as dramatic as a branding iron and she felt her heart pick up speed until she thought it might explode inside her.

'Not so fast.'

'I've answered all your questions, Alessandro!'

'What the hell was in it for you?'

'Nothing! I…just made a mistake! It was a long time ago. I was just a kid.'

'A kid of twenty and already hitched. I didn't think that kind of thing happened any more.'

'I told you…we were in love…' Chase looked away and

shook her hand free of his vice-like grip. 'We didn't see the point of waiting.'

'And your families both joined in the celebrations?'

She shrugged. 'He's dead now, anyway, so it doesn't matter whether they joined in the celebrations or not.'

'Spoken like a true grieving widow.' Why did he keep getting this feeling that something was out of kilter? Was his mind playing tricks on him? Had his ego been so badly bruised eight years ago that he would rather look for hidden meanings than take her very simple tale of treachery at face value?

'It's been years. I've moved on.'

'And no one else has surfaced on the scene to replace the late lamented?'

'Why is this all about me?' Chase belatedly thought that she might turn the spotlight onto him. If there was one thing to be said for going into law whilst simultaneously detaching yourself from most of the human race, it was that it did dramatic things to your confidence levels. Or maybe it was just her 'flight or fight' reflex getting an airing. She stared him squarely in the face and tried not to let the steady, speculative directness of his gaze get to her.

'What about *you*?' she asked coolly. 'We haven't said anything about what *you've* been up to…'

'What's there to say?' Alessandro relaxed back, angling his body so that he could cross his legs. She really did have a face that made for compulsive watching. It was exquisite, yet with a guarded expression that made you wonder what was going on behind the beautiful mask. Even as a much younger woman, she had possessed that sense of unique mystery that had fired his curiosity and kept it for the duration of their strange dalliance.

And now, yet again, he could feel his curiosity piqued.

'I'm an open book.' He spread his arms wide. 'I don't

hide who I am and I don't make a habit of leading anyone down the garden path.'

'And is there a special someone in *your* life? Is there a Mrs Moretti dusting and cleaning in a house in the country somewhere and a few little Moretti children scampering around outside? Or are you still only into the fast and furious relationship without the happy ending?'

'My, my. You've certainly become acid-tongued, Chase.'

Chase flushed. Yes she had. And there were times when she stood back and wondered if she really liked the person she had become. Not that she had ever been soft and fluffy, but now…

'I don't like being trampled.'

'And is that why you think I brought you here? To trample over you? Is that what you think I'm doing?'

Chase shrugged. 'Isn't it?'

'We're exchanging information. How could that possibly be described as trampling all over you? And, in answer to your question, there is no Mrs Moretti in a country house—and if there were, she certainly wouldn't be dusting or cleaning.'

'Because you have enough money to pay for someone to dust and clean for you. Are you still working twenty-four-seven? Surely you must have made enough billions by now to kick back and enjoy life?'

She used to listen, enraptured, as he'd told her about his working life: non-stop; on the go all the time. The lectures, he had said, were like comic relief, little windows of relaxation. She had teased him that, if giving lectures was his form of relaxation, then he would keel over with high blood pressure by the time he was thirty-five. She was annoyed to find herself genuinely curious and interested to hear what he had been up to. Having anything to do with Alessandro Moretti was even more hazardous now than it had been eight years ago.

'None of my business,' she qualified in a clipped voice. 'Am I free to go now?'

Alessandro's lips thinned. He had found out precisely nothing. None of his questions had been answered. His brain was telling him to walk away but some other part of him wanted more.

'Why did you decide to concentrate on pro bono cases?' He asked softly. 'Surely with a first-class degree, and law firms head-hunting you, there were far more profitable things to do?'

'I've never been interested in making money.' He had stopped attacking her and she realised that she had forgotten how seductive he could be when he was genuinely interested in hearing what she had to say. He would tilt his head to one side and would give the impression that every word she uttered was of life-changing importance.

'I'd always planned on becoming a lawyer, although the two other options that tempted me were Social Services and the police force.' She blushed, because she didn't think that she had confided that in anyone before—not that she did a lot of confiding anyway.

'Social Services? The police force?'

'So please don't accuse me of being materialistic.'

'I can't picture you as a social worker, even less a policewoman.'

'I should be getting back to work. I have a lot to do, and I'll have to visit the shelter later today and tell them what the outcome of my meeting with your company was. They'll be disappointed because they honestly don't want to move premises, not when they've been such a reliable fixture in the area for such a long time, and not when the majority of the women who use their services are fairly local to the area. A big place with a swimming pool and a games room in the middle of nowhere is no good for anyone.'

'What made the decision for you?'

Hadn't he been distracted from asking her personal questions? Having lowered her guard for three seconds, Chase now felt as though she was handing over state secrets to the enemy, and yet what was the big deal? Was she so defensive because Alessandro was on the receiving end of her confidences? And wasn't it possible that, the more secretive she was, the more curious he would become? She forced herself to relax and smile at him.

'The hours,' she confessed in a halting voice. 'I didn't want to think that I might be called out at any time of the day or night. I might work long hours at Fitzsimmons but I can control the hours I work.'

'Makes sense. More to the point, I suppose both other options would have involved an element of danger, and even more so for someone like you.'

'Someone like me?' Immediately, Chase bristled at the implied insult. 'And I suppose you're going to launch into another attack on me? More criticism of me that I'm a liar and a cheat? Although I have no idea how that would have anything to do with being in the police force or working for the council! I get it that you're angry and bitter about what happened between us, but attacking me isn't going to change any of that!'

'Actually,' Alessandro murmured, 'I meant that those two professions are the ones that are possibly least suited to a woman with your looks. You're sexy as hell; how would that have played out for you if you had found yourself in a dangerous situation…?' The lips he had never kissed and the body he had never touched…

Suddenly, his body jackknifed into sudden, shocking arousal. The sheer force of it took him by surprise. It pushed its way past his bitterness and anger and made a mockery of the answers he had told himself he demanded to hear. As his erection throbbed painfully against the zip of his trousers, his mind took flight in a completely different direction. He imagined her hand down there, her mouth wrapped around him…

Who the hell cared about answers when he was consumed with lust? He had to shift in the chair just to release some of the urgency that was becoming painful.

He was suffused with anger at his physical response to her. She represented everything he found most repellent, yet how was it that she could still manage to turn him on? Was his libido so wayward that it could defy cool judgement and rise to the challenge of the unavailable, the unacceptable…the out of bounds? He had never lost control when it came to any woman and he had dated some of the most spectacularly beautiful women in the world. So what the hell was going on here?

'I never gave that side of things any thought at all.' Chase was determined not to let that description of her take their conversation in a direction she most certainly didn't want.

Her voice was cool, Alessandro noted, yet her colour was up. And she couldn't meet his eyes. Now, wasn't *that* telling?

He knew that the last thing he should contemplate doing was to pay any credence to whatever her expression was saying or, more to the point, whatever his disobedient body was up to, and yet…

'You know what? I think I might like to see this shelter. Evaluate just how the land will play out for what I have in mind. I'm taking it you'll be my escort…?'

CHAPTER THREE

FOR THE FIRST time in years Chase felt helpless. Three days ago she had walked into the imposing glass building that housed AM Holdings with a simple mission: save the shelter. She had been in control—the career woman, successful in what she did, in command of the situation. She had hoped for a favourable outcome but, had there not been one, she would have left with a clear conscience—she would have done her best.

And now here she was, hanging around by the window in her house, peering out at regular intervals for Alessandro, who had made good on his request to be shown the shelter.

'What for?' she had demanded at the time. 'I don't see the point. You're just going to demolish it anyway so that you can put up a mall catering for rich people.'

'Be warned,' he had said, eyebrows raised, those midnight eyes boring straight through her, making her feel as though her whole body had been plugged into a socket. 'Do-gooders and preachers have a monotonous tendency to become self-righteous bores. Naturally, I have details of the land somewhere but I want to see for myself what the layout is. Since you're the one handling the deal, I can't imagine that would be a problem. Or is it? Does our past history make it a problem for you?'

Yes. Yes, it does, she had thought with rising desperation. 'No. Of course not. Why should it?' she had answered with an indifferent shrug.

So here she was now and she felt as though control was slipping out of her grasp. She knew that under normal circumstances a lapse in her self-control would be easily dealt with but with Alessandro…

Her frustration and anger was underlined by a darker, more insidious emotion, a swirl of excitement that scared her. It felt like a slumbering monster slowly reawakening. Even though she had taken care to dress as neutrally as possible, in a navy-blue suit that was the epitome of sexlessness—and an impractical colour, given the wall-to-wall blue summer skies and hot sunshine—she still felt horribly vulnerable as she hovered in the sitting room waiting for him to show up.

She had informed him that she would meet him at the premises, but he had insisted on collecting her.

'You can fill me in on the history of the place on the way,' he had said smoothly. 'Forewarned is forearmed.'

She had bitten her tongue and refrained from telling him that there was no point being forearmed when the net result would be a demolition derby. He was the guy with the purse strings and she had already seen first-hand how he could use that position to his own advantage. She had no desire to revive the ticking clock.

A long, sleek, black Jaguar pulled up outside the house just as she was about to turn away from the window and her attention was riveted at the sight of him emerging from the back seat, as incongruous in this neighbourhood as his car was.

He was dressed in pale-grey pinstriped trousers, which even from a distance screamed quality, and a white shirt, the sleeves of which he had rolled to the elbow.

For a few heart-stopping seconds, Chase found that she literally couldn't breathe, that she was holding her breath.

The mere sight of him was a full-on assault on all her senses. She watched as he looked around him, taking in his surroundings. She felt sure that this was the sort of neighbourhood he would be accustomed to telling his chauffeur to drive straight through and to make sure the car doors were locked. By no means was it in a dangerous part of London but neither was it upmarket. Well paid though she was, she wasn't so well paid that she could afford to buy a house in one of the trendier areas and, unlike many of her associates, she didn't have parents who could stick their hands in their pockets and treat her to one.

She dodged out of sight just as he turned to face the house and, when the doorbell rang, she took her time getting to it. Her heart was beating like a sledgehammer as she pulled open the door to find him lounging against the doorframe.

'Right. Shall we go?' she asked as her eyes slid away from his sinfully handsome face, returned to take a peek and slid away again. She gathered her handbag from where she had hung it on the banister and bent to retrieve her briefcase from the ground.

'In due course.' Alessandro stepped into the hallway and shut the front door behind him.

'What are you doing?'

'I'm coming in for a cup of coffee.'

'We haven't got time for that, Alessandro. The appointment has been made for ten-fifteen. With rush-hour traffic, heaven only knows how long it will take for us to get there.'

'Relax. I got my secretary to put back the visit by an hour.'

'You *what?*'

'So this is where you live.'

Chase watched in horror as he made himself at home, strolling to peer into the sitting room, then onwards to the kitchen, into which he disappeared.

'Alessandro…' She galvanised herself into movement and hurried to the kitchen, to find him standing in the centre doing a full turn. It was a generous-sized kitchen which overlooked a small, private garden. It had been a persuading factor in her purchase of the house. She loved having a small amount of outdoor space.

'Very nice.'

'This is not appropriate!'

'Why not? It's hardly as though I'm a stranger. Are you going to make me a cup of coffee?'

Chase gritted her teeth as he sat down. The kitchen was large enough for a four-seater table and it had been one of the first things she had bought when she had moved in three years previously. She had fallen in love with the square, rough, wooden table with its perimeter of colourful, tiny mosaic tiles. She watched as he idly traced one long finger along some of the tiles and then she turned away to make them both some coffee.

'Is this your first house?' Alessandro queried when she had finally stopped busying herself doing nothing very much at the kitchen counter and sat down opposite him.

He hadn't laid eyes on her in three days but he had managed to spend a great deal of time thinking about her and he had stopped beating himself up for being weak. So what if she had become an annoying recurring vision in his head? Wasn't it totally understandable? He had been catapulted back to a past he had chosen to lock away. Naturally it would be playing on his mind, like an old, scratched record returned to a turntable. Naturally *she* would be playing on his mind, especially when she had remained just so damned easy on the eye.

'What do you mean?' Everything about Alessandro Moretti sitting at her kitchen table made her jumpy.

'Is this the family home?'

'I have no idea what you're talking about.'

'The dearly departed… Is this the marital home?'

'No, it's not.' She looked down. 'Shaun and I… We, er, had somewhere else when we were together… When he died I rented for a couple more years until I had enough equity to put in as a deposit on this place.'

Alessandro thought of the pair of them, young love-birds renting together, while she had batted her eyelashes at him and played him for a fool. He swallowed a mouthful of instant coffee and stood up, watching as she scrambled to her feet.

'Are you going to give me a tour of the place?'

'There isn't much to see. Two bedrooms upstairs; a bathroom. You've seen what's down here. Shall we think about going?'

Alessandro didn't answer. He strolled out of the kitchen, glancing upstairs before turning his attention to the sitting room. Why was she so jumpy? She had been as cool as a cucumber eight years ago when she had walked out on him, so why was she now behaving like a cat on a hot tin roof? Guilt? Hardly. A woman who could conduct an outside relationship while married would never be prone to guilt. Or remorse. Or regret.

Perversely, the jumpier she seemed to be, the more intrigued he became. He shoved one hand in his trouser pocket, feeling the coolness of his mobile phone.

'For a cool-headed lawyer,' he mused as he stared round the sitting room, 'you like bright colours. Anyone would be forgiven for thinking that the decor here suggests a completely different personality.' He swung round to look at her as she hovered in the doorway, neither in the room nor out of it. 'Someone fun…vibrant.' He paused a fraction of a second. 'Passionate…'

Chase flushed, and was annoyed with herself, because she knew that that was precisely the response he had been courting. He was back and he was intent on playing with her like a cat playing with a mouse, knowing that all the danger and all the power lay exclusively in his hands.

'And yet,' Alessandro drawled as he prowled through the room before gazing briefly out of the window which overlooked the little street outside, 'there's something missing.'

'What?' The question was obviously reluctantly spoken. As he began to walk towards her, she felt panic rise with sickening force to her throat. All at once she was overcome with a memory of how desperately she had wanted him all those years ago. Her eyes widened and her mouth parted on a softly indrawn breath.

Getting closer and closer to her, Alessandro thought he could *touch* the subtle change in the atmosphere between them. It had become highly charged and, for the first time in a very long time, he felt sizzlingly *alive.* Not one of the catwalk-model beauties he had slept with over the past few years had come close to rousing this level of forbidden excitement. The immediacy of his response shocked him, all the more so because he recognised that the last time he had felt like this was when he had been in the process of being duped by the very same woman standing in front of him now. Hatred and revulsion were clearly inadequate protection against whatever it was she had that was now pushing an erection to the fore.

The bloody woman had been elusive then, for reasons which he had later understood, and she was elusive now, this time for reasons he couldn't begin to understand.

'Are you afraid of me?' he demanded harshly and Chase roused herself from the heated torpor that had engulfed her to stare up at him.

'What makes you think that I'm afraid of you?' She tried to insert some vigour into her voice but she could hear the sound of it—thin, weedy and defensive, all the things she didn't want him to imagine she was for a second.

'The way you're standing in the doorway as though I might make a lunge for you at any minute!'

'I can't imagine you would do any such thing!'

Couldn't she? It was precisely what he wanted to do: behave like a caveman and take her, because she was tempting the hell out of him!

'I'm afraid of what you could do.' She backtracked quickly as her mind threatened to veer down unexpected, unwelcome paths. 'You've already shown that you'd be willing to punish Beth because you… Because of me.'

'And yet here I am now. Do you think I'm the sort of man who reneges on what he's said? I've told you that I intend to pay the full, agreed price. I'll pay it.' Not afraid of him? *Like hell.* She might not be afraid of him, but he was certainly making her feel uncomfortable. Uncomfortable enough to try and shimmy further away from him.

He extended one lean hand against the wall, effectively blocking any further scarpering towards the front door. He could smell her hair. If he lowered his head just a little, he would feel its softness against his face. Of their own accord, his eyes drifted to the prissy blouse and the even prissier navy-blue jacket. He was well aware that she was breathing quickly, her breasts rising and falling as she did her utmost to keep her eyes averted.

Just as quickly he pushed himself away, retreating from her space, and he watched narrowly as she relaxed and exhaled one long breath.

He wasn't going to lose control. He had lost control once with her and he wasn't about to become the sort of loser who made a habit of ignoring life's lessons and learning curves.

'I was going to say…' He led the way to the front door and paused as she slung her handbag over her shoulder and reached for the case on the ground. 'There's something missing from your house.' He opened the door for her and stood back, allowing her to brush past him. 'Photos. Where are the pictures of the young, loving couple, from before your husband died? I thought I might have seen the happy pair holding hands and gazing adoringly up at one another…'

Chase walked towards the waiting car, head held high, but underneath the composed exterior she felt the ugly prickle of discomfort.

'We didn't do the whole church thing.'

'Who said anything about a church?'

'Why are you asking me all these questions?' she burst out as soon as they were in the car. She had kept her voice low but she doubted the driver would have heard anything anyway. A smoked-glass partition separated the front of the car from the back. Presumably it was completely soundproof. The truly wealthy never took chances when it came to being overheard, not even in their own cars. Deals could be lost on the back of an overheard conversation.

Alessandro shifted his muscular body to face her. 'Why are you getting so hot under the collar?'

'I…I'm not. I…I don't like to be surrounded by memories. I think it's always important to move on. There are photos of me and Shaun, just not on show. Do you want to talk about the shelter? I…I've brought all the relevant information with me. We can go over it on the way.' Sitting next to him in the back seat of this car induced the feeling of walls closing in. She fumbled with the clasp of her briefcase and felt his hand close over hers.

'Leave it.'

Chase snatched her hand away. 'I thought you wanted to pick me up so that we could talk about this deal.'

'I'm more interested in the lack of photos. So, none of the husband. Presumably you have albums stashed away somewhere? But none of your family either. Why is that?'

Chase flushed. The adoring middle-class parents who

lived in the country. She was mortified at how easily the lie had come to her all those years ago, but then she had been a kid and a little harmless pretence had not seemed like a sin.

Who wanted a rich, handsome guy to know that you have no family? That your mother had died from a drugs overdose when you were four and from that point on you'd been shoved from foster home to foster home like an unwanted parcel trying to find its rightful owner. How wonderful it had been to create a fictitious family, living in a fictitious cul-de-sac, who did normal things like taking an interest in the homework you were set and coming along to cheer at sports days, even if you trailed in last.

She had loved every minute of her storytelling until it had occurred to her that she had fallen in love with a man who didn't really know a thing about her. The fact that she had been married was just one of the many facts she had kept hidden. By then, it had been too late to retract any of what she had said, and she hadn't wanted to. She'd been enjoying their furtive meetings too much. Okay, so she knew that they would never come to anything, but she still hadn't wanted them to end.

And now…

'My parents…er…moved to Australia a few years ago.' She hated doing this now but for the life of her she didn't know what to do. At least, she thought, sending her non-existent parents on a one-way ticket to the other end of the world would prohibit him from trying to search them out.

Although, why on earth would he do that? The answer came as quickly as the question had: revenge. Find her weak spots and exploit them because he hated her for what he imagined she had done to him. She felt sick when she thought of the number of ways he could destroy her if he set his mind to it and if he had sufficient information in his possession.

'Really?'

'It was…um…always a dream of theirs.'

'To leave their only child behind and disappear halfway across the world?'

'People do what they do,' she said vaguely. 'I mean, don't *you* ever want to disappear to the other end of the earth?' Although she was making sure to stare straight ahead, she could feel his probing eyes on her, and she had to resist the temptation to lick her lips nervously.

'I disappear there quite often, as it happens. But only on business.'

Chase could think of nothing worse than travelling the globe in the quest for more and more money and bigger and bigger deals. Stability, security and putting down roots had always been her number one priority. She had managed to begin the process, and she shuddered to think of him pulling up any of the roots she had meticulously put down over the past few years.

'I'm surprised that after all these years you haven't become tired of trying to make up for your parents' excesses.' It slipped out before she could think and Chase instantly regretted the momentary lapse. The last thing she wanted to do was establish any kind of shared familiarity. 'My apologies,' she said stiffly. 'I shouldn't have said that.'

The reminder of just how much she knew about him underscored his bitterness with a layer of ice. He had never understood how that had managed to happen, how he had found himself telling her things he had never told anyone in his life before.

But then, she had been different. He had never met anyone like her in his life before. Still and yet wryly funny; guarded and yet so open in the way she gazed at him; composed and brilliant at listening. Between the inane yakking of the students—who, at the end of the day, were only a few years younger than him, even though he had been light years removed from them in terms of experience—and the pseudo-bored sophistication of the people he mixed with in his working life, she had been an oasis of peace. And, yes, he had told her things. For a relationship that struggled even to call itself a 'relationship', he had confided and, hell, where exactly had it got him?

He clenched his jaw grimly. 'I'm really not interested in psychobabble,' he told her.

'That's fair,' Chase returned. 'But if I'm not allowed to talk about *your* history then I don't see why you should talk about *mine*.' For starters, the last thing she needed was detailed questions about her so-called parents and where exactly they lived in Australia. And how dared he imply that they somehow didn't care about her simply because they had fulfilled their lifelong dream of emigrating? She almost felt sorry for them…

She half-grinned at that and Alessandro's eyes narrowed. What was going through her head? He had a fierce desire to know.

'So the shelter…' He interrupted whatever pleasant thought had made her smile.

'The shelter…' Chase breathed an inward sigh of relief because this was a subject she was more than happy to talk about. He ceased being a threat as she began to describe life at Beth's House. She smiled at some of the anecdotes about the women who came and went. She told him about the plans Beth had had for upgrading the premises, and then assured him that he could see for himself what she was talking about as soon as he got there. She told him that he had a heart of stone for wanting to knock it down to build, of all things, a stupid mall for people who had more money than sense, but found it was impossible to generate an argument because he hadn't taken her to task for voicing her opinion.

As a professional, a lawyer in charge of the brief, voicing opinions was not within her remit but she hadn't been able to help herself.

By the time they made it to the shelter, her eyes were bright and there was colour in her cheeks. More to the point, her guard was down. Alessandro felt that he was watching the years falling away. He wasn't about to be sucked into believing that she was anything but the liar she undoubtedly was, but he was certainly enjoying the hectic flush in her cheeks and the lively animation on her face.

They made it to the shelter on time. He immediately understood its potential for investment.

The large Victorian house, clearly in need of vast sums of money for essential repair, sat squarely in the midst of several acres of land. For somewhere that was accessible by bus and overland rail, it was a gem waiting to be developed.

The car swung through iron gates that were opened for them only after they had cleared security and they drove up to the house which was fronted by a circular courtyard, in the centre of which stood a non-functioning fountain.

'Beth was left this property by her parents,' Chase told him. 'It's another reason why she's so reluctant to sell. It was her childhood home. She may have converted it into the shelter, but there are a truck load of memories inside.'

'Is this when you begin to repeat your mantra that I have no heart and that my only aim in life is to make money at other people's expense?'

'If the cap fits…' Chase muttered under her breath in yet another show of unprofessionalism that would have had her boss mopping his brow with despair.

Alessandro raised his eyebrows and she had the grace to blush before stepping out of the car into the sunshine.

Alessandro was more than happy to follow her lead. He had never been to a place like this before. They were greeted at the door by Beth, who was in her sixties, a woman with long, grey hair tied back in a ponytail and a warm, caring face. Whatever she felt for the big, bad developer who was moving in to sweep her inheritance out from under her feet, she kept it well hidden.

'Some of the girls who come to us are in a terrible way,' she confided as they toured the house which was laid out simply but effectively inside. 'Chase knows that.'

'And that would be because…?'

'Because I've taken an interest in the place from the very start,' Chase said quickly. 'This sort of thing appeals to me. As I told you, I was very tempted to go into Social Services or the police force, some place where I would be able to do good for the community.'

Alessandro personally thought that it was priceless that she could come over all pious and saintly in his presence but he kept silent. He made all the right noises as he was shown through the house and introduced to girls who looked unbearably young, many of whom had nowhere else to go and were either pregnant or with a child.

'I try and keep them busy,' Beth told him as they went from room to room. 'Most of them don't see the point of continuing their education and it's very difficult for a fifteen-year-old to go to classes when they have a baby to look after. Many of my dear friends are teachers and volunteer to hold classes for them. It's truly remarkable the goodness that exists within us.'

Alessandro's eyes met Chase's over the older woman's head and his lips twisted into a cynical smile. 'It's not a trait I see much of in my line of business,' he said.

'I'm sure,' Beth concurred with a sad shake of her head. 'Now, Chase tells me that you're a very busy man.'

'And yet,' Chase inserted blandly, 'he's managed to make time to come here and see what you're all about. Although, I guess that mostly has to do with him judging the potential for knocking down the house and developing the land as soon as the money changes hands.'

Alessandro was cynical enough to appreciate the underhand dig. No one could accuse her of giving up without a fight. Their eyes tangled and he gave a slight smile of amused understanding of where she was heading with that incendiary statement.

'I will personally see to it that your…operation is transferred to suitable premises,' he affirmed, raking fingers through his dark hair.

'Not the same. Is it, Beth?'

'I will certainly miss the old place,' Beth agreed. 'It may not seem much to you, Mr Moretti, but this is really the only house I've ever known. I've never married, never left the family house. You must think me a silly old woman, but I shall find it very difficult to move on. Well, in truth—and I haven't said this to you, Chase, and you must promise me that you won't breathe a word to anyone else—my thoughts are with retiring from the whole business once I move on. Of course, I shall make sure that some of the money I get from the sale goes towards another shelter—perhaps smaller than this—and Frank and Anne will run it.'

'Frank and Anne?' Alessandro made a point of avoiding the scathing criticism in Chase's eyes. He had absolutely nothing to feel bad about. He knew for a fact that there were vultures hovering over the place, waiting to pick it to pieces, and those vultures would not have parted with nearly as much cash as he was prepared to.

'My dear friends. They help me here. As for me, perhaps a retirement place by the coast… So, I expect you would like to see the land, Mr Moretti? There's a lot of it. My parents were both keen gardeners. Sadly, I haven't had the money to look after it the way it deserves, but if the place is to be redeveloped then I'm sure you won't find that a problem. Chase tells me you have grand plans for it to be an upmarket mall.'

Alessandro marvelled that 'an upmarket mall' could be made to sound like 'the tower of Babel', although when he looked at the older woman there was no bitterness on her face.

'It will bring a great deal of useful traffic to the community.'

So he made money. It was what he did. It was what he had always done. And he was still doing it. He frowned as he remembered Chase's barbed comment about his lifestyle.

He had enough money to retire for the rest of his life and still be able to afford what most people could only ever dream of. So was he trying to make up for his parents' excesses? He was angry and frustrated that he should even be thinking along these lines. His parents were long gone and he had barely known them. How could he have, when, from a toddler, he had been in the care of a succession of nannies who had all fallen by the wayside in favour of boarding school abroad?

His parents had both been products of ridiculously wealthy backgrounds and their marriage had provided them with a joint income that they had both happily and irresponsibly squandered. Untethered by any sense of duty, and riding high on the hippie mentality that had been sweeping through Italy at the time, they had zoned out on recreational drugs, held lavish parties, travelled to festivals all over the world and bought houses which they had optimistically called 'communes' where people could 'get in touch with themselves'. And then, to top it all off, they had seen fit to throw away yet more of their inheritance on a series of ill-advised schemes involving organic farming and the import of ethnic products, all of which had crashed and burned.

Alessandro, barely through with university, had had to grasp what remained of the various companies and haul them back into profit when his parents had died in a boating accident in the Caribbean. Which he had done—in record time and with astounding success.

So what if he had learnt from his parents that financial security was the most important thing in life? So what if nothing and no one had ever been allowed to interrupt that one, single, driving ambition?

A woman in whom he had once rashly confided things that should have been kept to himself was certainly not going to make him start questioning his ethos.

Beth was now chatting amicably about the wonderful advantages of the place being developed, which would bring much-needed jobs to the community. To Alessandro's finely tuned ears, it sounded like forced enthusiasm. It was clear that she hated the thought of leaving the house, and he couldn't help wondering what someone who had always been active in community life in London would do in the stultifying boredom of the seaside.

It was after midday by the time they were standing outside the house saying their goodbyes. His chauffeur had returned for them but Chase pointedly made no move in the direction of the car.

'I'll make my own way back,' she said politely.

'Get in.' Alessandro stood to one side and then sighed with exasperation as she continued to look at him in stubborn silence. 'It's baking hot out here,' he said, purposefully invading her space by standing too close to her. 'And that outfit isn't designed for warm weather.'

'I'll take my chances on avoiding sunstroke.'

'Which is something I would rather not have on my conscience.'

'You don't have a conscience!'

'And you do?'

Chase looked at him with simmering resentment. *He* didn't look all hot and bothered. *He* looked as fabulous, cool and composed as he always did. Plus, he had charmed his way into Beth's affections. She could tell. He hadn't come on too strong, he had pointed out all the benefits of selling the place but in a perfectly reasonable way that no one would have been able to dispute. He was just so… damned *persuasive*! She hated it. And she hated the way she had found herself staring at him surreptitiously, hated the way her imagination had started playing tricks on her, hated the way she had had to fight against being seduced by the dark, deep, velvety tones of his voice.

'You can drop me to the bus stop. It's about a mile from here.'

'Are you going back to your office? Perhaps I could go in, meet all these people you work with… Tell your boss what a great job you've done even though the shelter will be sold. At least you've got me to thank for a reasonably happy Beth.'

'She's not happy.' Chase slid into the back seat, barely appreciating the terrific air conditioning as she grappled with the horror of having him invade her work space as well as having invaded her house. 'And I'm going home, as a matter of fact. I have work I can do there.'

'I've noticed that you try and avoid looking at me as much as possible,' Alessandro said softly. 'Why is that?'

As challenges went, that was about as direct as they came. *Avoid looking at him?* She wanted to laugh at the irony because all she seemed to do was look at him—it was just that she was careful with her staring. She looked at him now and the silence seemed to go on for ever as he gazed right back at her. Her mouth had gone dry and, although she knew that she should be breaking this yawning silence with a suitably innocuous remark, her mind refused to play along.

When he reached out and trailed one finger along her lips, she gasped with shock. There was a sudden, ferocious roaring in her ears and she couldn't breathe. All the strategies she had adopted to keep him at arm's length, to make him know that there was nothing whatsoever between them now aside from a brief, dubious past that no longer meant a thing, disappeared like mist on a hot summer's day.

She was no longer the lawyer with her life under control and he was no longer public enemy number one, the guy who could ruin everything she had built for herself in one fell swoop. She was a woman and he was a man and she still, against all rhyme or reason, wanted him with every incomprehensible, yearning ounce of her being.

'What are you doing?' She finally found her voice and pulled back.

Alessandro smiled. If he had had any doubts that she was still attracted to him, then he had none now. 'Maybe you're right,' he murmured, obediently removing his hand and observing her neutrally. 'Your friend really doesn't want to leave her home. The memories…the experiences… I don't see a bungalow on the coast cutting it, do you?'

'No.' Chase glared at him suspiciously. Her lips were burning from where he had touched them but she refused to cool them with her fingers.

'So I have an interesting proposal to put to you. You'd like me to believe that you're all bleeding heart and caring for the defenceless. Well, how would you like to prove it?'

CHAPTER FOUR

CHASE DIDN'T ANSWER immediately. Alessandro slid back the partition and told the driver to deliver them to a well-known French restaurant. By the time that sank in, the car had already altered course.

'What the heck do you think you're doing?'

'We're going to discuss my proposal over food. It's lunchtime.'

'And I've told you that I need to get back to do some work! Besides, I can't imagine what sort of proposal you have for me that involves you kidnapping me!'

'I like your use of language. Colourful.'

Chase was still burning from where his finger had touched her lips. Her mouth tingled.

'What made your friend decide to go into the good Samaritan business?'

Chase looked at him with unbridled suspicion. He was leaning indolently against the door and she got the feeling that it was all the better to see her. Like the big, bad wolf in the fairy story. 'I don't know what good it will do for you to hear Beth's potted history.'

'I've never known anyone who erects so many obstacles to complicate a perfectly harmless conversation.'

'That's because everyone kowtows to you, I imagine,' Chase offered ungracefully. While he was supremely relaxed, legs slightly open, one arm along the back of the seat, the other hanging loosely over his thigh, she was as tense as a block of wood. Her legs were tightly pressed together. Her lips were tightly compressed. Her fingers were interlinked and white at the knuckles.

'Rich people seem to have that effect,' she continued, avoiding his speculative eyes. 'I've seen it. They like throwing their weight around and they take it for granted that everyone is going to agree with everything they say.'

'You're getting all hot and bothered over nothing,' Alessandro murmured with mild amusement. 'The food at this restaurant is second to none. Have you been there? No? Then you should be looking forward to the experience. So why don't you relax? Tell me about your friend.'

'You didn't seem that interested in her when you were downgrading the price of the place by a thousand pounds per minute.'

'That was before I met her.'

Every argument she engineered seemed to crash into a brick wall. He wasn't interested in arguing with her. She, on the other hand, felt driven to keep arguing because something inside her was telling her that, if she didn't, she might find herself in dangerously unchartered territory. She might start remembering how funny he could be, how thoughtful, how engaging.

'She obviously comes from a fairly wealthy background,' Alessandro murmured encouragingly. 'And yet the road she decided to travel down wasn't exactly the predictable one.'

When he had first laid eyes on Chase after eight years, he had been shocked. And hard on the heels of that shock had come rage and bitterness. It seemed that he had badly underestimated the effect she had had on him. He hadn't put her behind him after all. Had he succeeded in doing that, he would have felt nothing but indifference and contempt. So, yes, revenge had been an option but why make a third party suffer? Weren't there other ways of handling a situation that had landed in his lap?

Rage and bitterness were corrosive emotions and there was one very good way of permanently eliminating them. He smiled with slow, deliberate intent.

Chase took note of that smile and wondered what the heck was going on.

'She hasn't had a…normal upbringing,' she said reluctantly. 'I know this because I knew her before this whole business with the shelter cropped up. Actually, she came to me when she was approached with your company's interference because we were already friends.'

'Interference? I'll overlook your take on my generous offer to buy her out. How did you become friends? Oh no, don't tell me—you were drawn to her because of your "care in the community" approach to life.'

'I'm glad you think it's funny to want to help other people!'

'I don't. I think it's admirable. Like I said, I just find the sentiments hard to swallow when they're coming from you.'

'If I'm such an awful person, why are you taking me out to lunch? Why didn't you let me find my own way back? The sale's agreed. Your legal team could take it from here on in.'

'But then I would miss out on the pleasure of watching you.'

Chase flushed and wondered whether he was being serious or not. She told herself that she didn't care and squashed the unwanted sliver of satisfaction it gave her when she thought of him watching her and *enjoying* it. Suddenly, it felt safer to talk about Beth than to sit in silence, as he looked at her, and speculate on all sorts of things that threw her into confusion.

'Her parents were both really well off,' she blurted out,

licking her lips nervously and wishing he would just stop looking at her in that pensive, brooding way that made the hairs on the back of her neck stand on end. 'They were missionaries. Beth says that as though it's the most normal thing in the world.'

She began to relax and half-smiled as she remembered the conversation they had had years ago when she had first met her. 'I mean, they didn't want to convert anyone, but they wanted to help people in the third world. They rented out their house, which is now the shelter, and took themselves off to Africa where they spent their own money on various irrigation and building projects. In fact, there's a plaque dedicated to them in one of the little villages over there.'

'Good people.' Alessandro thought of his own feckless parents and marvelled at the different ways money could be spent.

'They returned to London to live when Beth was a child. I think they wanted her educated over here. Maybe they thought that they had done what they had set out to do. At any rate, they found that they couldn't just do nothing once they'd come back, so they did lots of volunteer work at various places. They were both in their fifties by then. They'd had Beth when they were quite old. Beth went to university and studied to become an engineer, but found herself drawn to helping others, and when her parents died and she inherited the house and land, the stocks and shares and stuff, she turned the house into a shelter and hasn't looked back.'

'So effectively it's really the only house she's ever lived in and the only work she's ever done.'

'Yes. So there you have it. I don't suppose you can really understand what makes someone like Beth tick.'

'Do me a favour and stop trying to pigeon-hole me because I happen to have a bit of money.'

'A bit of money? You're as rich as Croesus.' They were now in front of the restaurant and Chase stared down at her formal working suit in dismay. 'I don't feel comfortable dining in a place like this wearing a suit.'

'Don't wear the jacket and undo the top three buttons of the shirt.'

'I beg your pardon?' She looked at him, her cheeks bright red, and he grinned at her. A full-on charming grin that knocked her sideways. It was that same grin that had turned her life on its head eight years ago and had made her continue to see him even though everything in her had been screaming at her to stop.

'You heard me.' He stepped out of the car and leaned through to give his driver instructions; when he straightened, it was to see that the prissy jacket, at least, had been left behind in the car.

'What about the buttons?' he asked, with the same sexy grin that made her toes curl and her skin feel tight and prickly.

He didn't give her time to think about it. With their eyes still locked, he undid the offending buttons. The softness of her skin under the starchy top… The glimpse of a cleavage… His breath caught sharply in his throat, mimicking hers.

'Don't do that!' Chase clasped the top and stumbled back a few steps.

'Much better. After you?'

Chase barely took note of the restaurant as they were ushered inside. She had been to a few fancy places since she had started working at Fitzsimmons. Her inclination to stare in awe had thankfully subsided. Nor was her mind in full working order just at the moment, not when her body was still in a state of heightened response at that intimate gesture of his undoing those buttons as though…as though she was his; as though they were the lovers they never, actually, ever had been.

'You said you had a proposal to put to me,' was the first thing she said tightly as soon as they were seated.

Alessandro perused the menu and made a few helpful suggestions which Chase ignored.

'This isn't a social occasion,' she said, choosing the first thing off the menu and shaking her head when he tried to entice her into a glass of wine.

'But it could be,' he returned smoothly. 'Couldn't it?'

'What do you mean?'

'I mean that eight years ago you were a married woman, albeit without my knowledge. Now, you're not. Your husband is no longer around and, unless you have another one stashed up your sleeve somewhere…?'

Caught unawares, Chase laughed shortly. 'Marriage isn't an institution I'll be going near again. Been there, done that, got the tee-shirt.'

Alessandro maintained a steady smile but his jaw hardened. 'Still in mourning?' he asked softly.

'Too wrapped up with my career,' Chase answered steadily.

'You haven't answered my question, but no matter. It really doesn't make any difference to the proposal I have in mind.' So she was still wrapped up in the ex. Why else would she have been at pains to avoid his question? He harked back to his image of the man, good-looking in a thuggish sort of way, her type of guy.

And yet, wrapped up or not in the past, she was still affected by *him*. He knew that with some highly developed sixth sense. As affected by him as he was, unfortunately, affected by her. She was an itch that needed to be scratched and he intended to do just that. Scratch the itch, and he would get her out of his system once and for all.

'So what's your proposal?' Had she ordered crab

mousse? It seemed so, as one was placed in front of her. She tucked into it without appetite.

'Do you get as personally wrapped up with all your clients as you do with this particular one?' Alessandro watched as she toyed with the starter in front of her.

'I told you. I knew her before… She's been a friend for years.'

'She's in her sixties.'

'What does age have to do with anything?' Chase looked at him defensively. Yes, she knew where this was going. Why was a young girl in her twenties friends with a woman in her sixties? Of course, age was no barrier to friendship. Many young people had friends who were much older than they were. What was the big deal? But Beth was one of her few friends, one of the few people in whom she had confided to some extent.

'Nothing. It's laudable. Although…'

'Although what? I suppose you're going to tell me that my friends should all be young and frivolous? That I should be spending my free time going to clubs and drinking instead of hanging out with a woman old enough to be my mother?'

'Although…isn't there something that suggests you shouldn't be working for someone with whom you're personally involved? I wasn't going to lecture you on hanging out with anyone. You choose your own friends, Chase. Interesting, however, that you never seemed to have a lot of those when I knew you eight years ago.'

'I…' She stared at him and, as their eyes tangled, she had the strangest sensation that he could see what was going on in her head. 'How would you know what friends I had or didn't have? You were only around part of the time. We met occasionally. You didn't know what I did in my spare time.'

Alessandro sat back as their food was placed in front

of them. He was surprised to see that he had eaten his starter although he couldn't even remember what he had ordered. She could barely meet his eyes and, again, he had the strangest feeling that there was something going on which he couldn't quite see.

He cursed himself for even being curious. 'True,' he concurred. 'And yet I remember a couple of occasions when kids from your course came up to you. You barely acknowledged them. Once they asked you if you were going to a party and you turned white and got rid of them as soon as you could.' The memory came from nowhere, as though it had been lurking there, just waiting to be aired.

'I…I had a husband.'

Alessandro found that he didn't like thinking about her husband. In fact, the thought of that shaved head, the tattoos, set his teeth on edge.

'Who would have been the same age as you were. Practically a teenager.'

It struck him that that was one of the things that had drawn him to her, the fact that she hadn't acted like a typical teenager. She had been old beyond her years in ways he couldn't quite pin down.

'I've never been into clubs and partying.'

'Never?'

'Why the thousand and one questions, Alessandro?' Her cheeks were bright red. Once upon a time she had actually enjoyed going out. She must have been fourteen or fifteen at the time, unsupervised, hanging out with older kids because most of the kids her age had had some form of parental control.

Schoolwork had been a breeze. She'd never had much need to bury her head in books. Absorbing information had come naturally to her. Oh yes, she had had plenty of time to go to clubs and parties. She frowned and wondered now whether she actually had enjoyed those parties, the dancing, the dim lights…and the confused, angry feeling that she shouldn't be there, that there should be someone in her life who cared enough to try and stop her.

'We're here. Why don't you just tell me what you want to say?'

'How does saving your friend's house sound to you?'

'Saving her house? What are you talking about?' Chase barely noticed that the starters had been removed, to be replaced with yet more exquisite food which she couldn't remember ordering. Despite having said no, her wine glass had been filled, and with a small shrug she sipped some of the cold white wine which tasted delicious. 'Are you going to build your mall around it?'

'Somehow I don't think that people on a quest for designer shoes would feel comfortable having to circumnavigate a shelter for women in need of help, do you?'

Chase thought about that and laughed. It was the first truly genuine laugh he had heard from her since they had met again and, God, how well he remembered the sound of it. Even back then, she hadn't laughed a lot, and when she had it was the equivalent of the sun coming out from behind a cloud. It was exactly the same now and he looked at her with rampant male appreciation.

'I know.' She grinned and leaned towards him confidingly. 'But wouldn't it be a great ploy? They'd all feel so guilty that they would contribute bags of money just to clear their conscience before they went to the shop next door to buy the designer shoes! Beth would never have any financial problems in her life again!'

'It would certainly be a solution of sorts to her financial problems,' Alessandro concurred.

'But you don't mean that, do you?' Her laughter subsided. She nibbled at the edges of her food and decided not to bother trying to second-guess what he had brought her here for.

'Not quite what I had in mind but the image was worth it just to hear the sound of your laugh.'

'Then what?' She ignored the tingling those words produced inside her. 'Will it involve getting any lawyers in? I can't honestly make any far-reaching decisions without reference to my boss.'

'How will he feel when you tell him that you'd had no option but to sell the place to me?' Alessandro asked curiously and Chase gave it some thought.

'A favourable outcome would have been for our client to hang on to the premises. The truth, however, is that our clients don't earn the firm money. The big money comes from our corporate and international clients. Intellectual property lawyers, patent lawyers, even some family lawyers…they earn the big money. I'm just a little cog subsidised by the big-fee lawyers, and I'm there because Fitzsimmons is a morally ethical law firm that believes in putting back some of what they take.'

Alessandro wasn't interested in hearing a long speech on the moral values of Fitzsimmons. 'Wonderful,' he said neutrally. 'But this particular decision won't require involvement from anyone else in your firm.'

'Okay.'

'Nor is it illegal.' Alessandro read the suspicion in her eyes and looked at her with wry amusement. 'However, yes, it will involve the house remaining in your friend's possession. More than that, what if I told you that I would be prepared to pay off all her debts and inject sufficient cash to make sure she can keep the shelter going for a very long time to come?'

Chase gaped at him. For a few seconds, she honestly believed that she had misheard what he had said. Then she thoughtfully closed her knife and fork, wiped her mouth with her linen serviette and searched his face to see whether this was some way of making a fool of her.

'So Beth…' she said slowly, giving him ample time to cut her short and rubbish what she thought he had said, 'gets to keep the house, plus you pay off her debts, plus you put money into renovating and updating the place… am I getting it right?'

'That would be about the size of it.'

'And you would do this because…?' Brow furrowed, she suddenly smiled at him with genuine delight. 'I know why. You were impressed with what you found at the shelter, weren't you? I don't suppose you were expecting it to be as well run as it was. Beth spares no effort when it comes to doing good for those girls. It's hard to go there and not be moved by what you find. I'm so pleased, Alessandro.' She reached out impulsively and covered his hand with hers.

Alessandro looked at the shining glow on her face and was extremely pleased with himself for being the one to put it there.

'Can I call and tell her?' Chase asked excitedly. 'No, perhaps I'd better not do that.' She flashed him an apologetic smile. 'You'll have to forgive the lawyer in me, but we'll have to get this all signed on the dotted line. But, once she knows, she'll be over the moon. Between you and me, I don't honestly think she was looking forward to a quiet retirement by the seaside.'

'So you agree with me that this is a good idea?'

'Of course I do! I'd be a fool not to.' Even with her defences up, knowing how he felt about her after what she had done to him, she knew that there was a blazingly good streak in him. Those lectures he had given had been given for free, and he had taken considerable time out to individually help some of the students, had actually offered internships to a couple of them. He hadn't just been as sexy as hell, he had shown her a glimpse of humanity that she had never seen before and that, amongst other things, had roped her in and kept her tethered in a place she had known was desperately dangerous.

'Naturally, there's no such thing as a free lunch in life.' Alessandro shook his head ruefully, the very picture of a man who regrets that there wasn't. 'I wish I could say that I was the perfect philanthropist, but you have to understand that all this will cost me a small fortune.'

The smile died on her face. The bill was brought to them and she automatically reached for her bag but it had been settled before she could rummage out her wallet and pay her fair share. 'Of course it will,' she agreed coolly. 'And you'll want to be repaid for your largesse. Will your rates be competitive?'

'Shall we go?'

Chase could feel disappointment rising inside her as he waited for her to gather her things, standing aside so that she could precede him out of the restaurant. Once outside, she didn't bother with her stupid jacket. He had been right when he had remarked that it was impractical for the weather.

What had he been playing at? Stringing her along with all manner of empty promises only to yank them all back at the last minute? Didn't he realise that, if Beth had wanted to borrow money so that she could clear her debts and get the shelter really going, she would have gone to the bank? Of course, Chase thought uncomfortably, she *had* tried that some time ago but to no avail. She simply hadn't had the collateral to get a loan of the size she required, even though the bank manager had known her parents. Money was just not being lent, not to ventures that had nothing to gain. Had Alessandro checked that out himself and come to the conclusion that he could provide her with the money but jack up the interest rates?

'I really believed you for a minute,' she simmered, barely noticing that she was being ushered into the back seat of his car. 'I really thought that you had been so impressed by what you saw that you decided to do the right thing. I really thought that there was a part of you that was the same guy who gave internships to those girls years ago, and the same guy who put in extra time helping that little group of Asian students through their language barriers with some of their papers.'

'You remember. Those girls have been promoted several times. One left a year ago to have a baby and returned a few months ago to resume work. Two of the Chinese students work in my Hong Kong offices.'

'You kept in touch with them.' She fought against the pull of a connection that threatened her valued self-control. She severed the incipient connection. 'Where are we going?'

'To discuss my proposal further. Out of public earshot.'

'Beth can't afford to pay you back for a loan.' Back to business, but her mind was still straying dangerously close to memories of the man she had once been so irresistibly drawn to—the man she knew still existed even if those complex sides, revealed all those years ago, would never again get an airing in her presence.

'Whoever mentioned loans?'

'You're confusing me, Alessandro.'

'Ditto,' he murmured under his breath. He looked at her in silence, his searing attraction laced with a poignant familiarity that wasn't doing his libido any favours, until she shifted uncomfortably and took notice of her surroundings. They were away from the hustle and bustle.

'And you haven't said where we're going. This isn't the way back to my house.'

'Well spotted. It's the way to mine.'

'What?' Chase immediately felt her pulses begin to race. She didn't want to be here, in this car! Far less heading to his place, wherever that was! He had just pulled a cheap trick, whatever he had said about his offer not being a loan. He had really shown his true colours, aside from which she knew that she should steer clear of him. But the memory of how much she had craved to see where he lived eight years ago slammed into her with the force of a freight train. 'Let me out of this car *immediately*.'

'Calm down.'

'I'm *perfectly* calm.'

'You're as perfectly calm as a volcano on the point of eruption. Relax. We'll be there in ten minutes.'

Chase felt ill at the thought of stepping foot into his private space. She had never thought that she would see him again and, now that she had, she should be laying down clear boundaries. Instead, the lines were blurring. He had come to her house, seen the way she lived, formed his opinions. Now she was going to his.

She watched with growing panic as the sleek, black car manoeuvred through quiet streets, finally turning into an avenue through imposing black wrought-iron gates. The houses here were beyond spectacular. No superlative could do justice to the pristine white-and-cream facades, the ornate foliage, the lush greenery, the air of indecently wealthy seclusion. The cars were all top of the range, high end.

So this was where he lived. Never in her wildest, twenty-year-old's dreams could she have come up with this.

'I'm not comfortable with this,' she said automatically as his driver opened the passenger door for her.

'I wasn't comfortable conducting a private conversation in a public place.'

'There was nothing private about our conversation. It was a business deal.' But she couldn't help staring at the enormous house in front of her, the perfectly shaped shrubs on either side of the black door, the highly polished brass of the knocker. Nor could she help feeling, in some deep, dark part of her, that their conversation had been threaded with undercurrents that were anything but businesslike.

'I love the way you constantly argue with me,' Alessandro remarked drily as he opened the front door and stood aside so that she brushed past him. 'It's refreshing. You did that eight years ago as well. And it was refreshing then.'

There had been times, countless times, when he had just wanted to scoop her to him and silence those feisty arguments with his mouth…just kiss them away. But he had been prepared to bide his time. He had been prepared to do way too much to attain the eventual goal of just having her. She had taught him the art of patience, damn fool that he had been.

Chase didn't say anything. She was too busy being impressed. It wasn't just the size but the pristine perfection: marble flooring, the colour of pale honey, was broken by silky rugs. The paintings on the walls varied in size but were recognisable—who on earth had paintings on their walls that were *recognisable*? The impressive staircase leading up gave onto a landing which was dominated by a massive stained-glass window that did magical things to the sunlight filtering through it.

She came back to planet Earth to find that Alessandro was watching her, hands in his pockets.

'You have a beautiful place,' she said politely.

Alessandro dutifully looked around him, as though taking stock of where he lived for the first time, then he shrugged. 'It works for me. Come through.'

'I honestly don't see why you couldn't have laid out your terms and conditions for this so-called "not a loan" at the restaurant.' But she followed as he led the way towards a kitchen that looked as though it had never been used. He didn't do cooking; she remembered him telling her that way back when.

'Have you *ever* used this kitchen?' she asked, perching on one of the top-of-the-range chrome and leather bar stools by the counter and watching as he attempted to make sense of the complicated coffee machine.

'You don't want coffee, do you?' he eventually asked, turning to glance at her over his shoulder.

'If I did, would you be able to figure out how that thing works?'

'Unlikely.'

'Tea would be nice.' She hadn't appreciated just how rich he was. These were the surroundings of a man to whom money was literally no object. She bristled when she thought of him holding her to ransom by reducing his offer for the shelter just because he could.

'I'm very good with a kettle and some tea bags.' He hunted them down, opening and closing cupboards. 'I come in here very rarely,' he offered by way of explanation. 'I have a housekeeper who makes sure it's stocked and a chef who does all my cooking on the occasions when I happen to be in.'

'Lucky you.'

There wasn't a single woman on the planet, Alessandro thought, who would have offered that sarcastic response when confronted with the reality of his wealth. 'You don't mean that.'

'You're right. I don't.' She took the cup of tea from him. The cup was fine-bone china, weirdly shaped, with an art deco design running down one side. When she thought of him trying and failing to work out how his high-tech appliances worked, she could feel a smile tugging the corners of her mouth, but there was no way that she would be seduced by any windows of vulnerability in him.

'Why do you have all these gadgets in here if you don't cook and barely use the kitchen?'

'I remain eternally optimistic.'

Chase wished he wouldn't do that, wouldn't undermine

her defences with his sense of humour. She didn't want to remember how he had always been able to make her laugh. She didn't want him to make her laugh now.

'Well, now we're here, maybe you could explain this business with the shelter?'

Alessandro looked at her. He wondered what it was about her that just seemed to capture his imagination and hold it to ransom.

'You have no idea what goes through me when I think of what you did eight years ago,' he murmured.

'You brought me here so that you could talk about that?' Chase fidgeted uncomfortably. She wanted to drag her disobedient eyes away from him but somehow she couldn't.

'But the past belongs in the past. What's the good dredging it up every two seconds? The best thing I could do right now is send you on your not-so-merry way, out of my life once and for all. Unfortunately, I find that there's something holding me back.'

'What?' It was a barely whispered response. She cleared her throat and did her utmost to remember that this was just an opponent whom she happened to have known a long time ago. It didn't work. She still found herself hanging onto his every word with shamefully bated breath, watching him watching her, and letting those deep, dark looks penetrate every fibre of her being. Dampness pooled shamefully between her legs, physical proof of something she was loath to admit, and her nipples tingled, sensitive and taut against her lacy bra. 'What's holding you back?' She shifted, felt her slippery wetness making her panties uncomfortable.

'You.' Alessandro allowed that one word to ferment in the lengthening silence between them until it was bursting with significance.

'I have no idea what you're talking about.'

'Of course you do,' he drawled smoothly. 'We can both

waste a little time while I indulge your desire to feign ignorance but what would be the point? We'll end up getting to the same place eventually. Despite what happened between us, despite the fact that my levels of respect for you are lamentably non-existent, I find that I'm still sexually attracted to you. And I wouldn't be telling you this now if I didn't know that it was a two-way street.

'And don't bother trying to deny it. I've seen the way you look at me when you think my attention is somewhere else and I've seen the way you respond whenever I get within a two-foot radius of you. We had it once and we have it again. It's a shame but…' He shrugged with graceful elegance.

'You're…you're mad…' Her words said one thing; her treacherous body however, was, singing a different refrain.

'Am I? I don't think so.'

Chase watched, mesmerised, as he slowly stood up and breached the short distance separating them to plant his hands on either side of her chair, locking her into place so that she could only raise her eyes upwards to stare at him. She could feel the pulse in her neck beating wildly, a physical giveaway that every word he was saying struck home.

'I'm the lawyer working for Beth; sure, we know each other…' The word faltered and died in her throat as he cupped her cheek with his hand and stroked it with his thumb.

Years ago, their chaste relationship had pulsated with unexplored passion and unspoken, untested lust. Now, as his hand remained on her cheek, she shuddered and resisted the urge to sink into the caress.

'Please, Alessandro, don't.'

'Your body is telling me something different.'

'I don't want to start any kind of relationship with you.'

'Relationship?' Alessandro queried huskily. 'Who's talking about a relationship? I could no more have a relationship with you than I could with a deadly snake. No, I'm not interested in a relationship. I'm interested in having sex with you, plain and simple. Just like you're interested in having sex with me. Don't you want to touch what you spent months staring at eight years ago? Don't you want to finish what you started? I do. A lot.'

Chase opened her mouth to tell him to get lost but nothing emerged. His cool, brilliant dark eyes held her in a trance even though she knew that every word that left that perfect mouth was offensive and insulting.

And yet…her imagination was going crazy. The fantasies she had had of him touching her all those years ago sprang from the box into which they had been firmly locked and attacked her on all fronts. She weakened at the thought of his fingers stroking the wetness between her legs, his mouth kissing the twin peaks of her breasts, nipping the tight buds of her nipples, suckling on them while he continued to stroke her dampness…

'So here's the deal.' Alessandro was finding it hard to contain his excitement at the prospect of netting the prey that had once escaped him and putting to bed, once and for all, feelings that had no place in his life. Her skin was like satin beneath his fingertips. 'You sleep with me for as long as I want you to and the shelter stays. Renovated, updated and modernised. Your friend's debts will be cleared.'

'You want to *pay* me for services rendered?'

'I want to take what you want to give. In return, you get the shelter. And please don't try and tell me that you don't want to touch me. You do.' His mouth met hers and Chase braced her hands on his shoulders, determined to push him away. But instead she was horrified to find that she was caressing him; that her mouth was returning his kiss with equal urgency; that she was sinking into him like a person starved of nourishment; that she was whimpering, little mewling sounds that shocked and excited her in equal measure and, worse, when he finally pulled back that the sudden space between them felt cold and unwelcome.

'I think I've proved my point.' There was a betraying unsteadiness in his voice. He might not like her or respect her but, God, did he want her. More than anything or anyone. 'Let's finish this business. A couple of weeks, tops, and you can disappear back to whatever life you have, having made your friend a very happy bunny.'

Chase had withdrawn and was rising to her feet, arms tight around her body.

'I'll never do that, Alessandro!'

Alessandro shrugged and tried to wrestle back his self-control, even though just watching her was affecting him in ways he could barely quantify. 'You have forty-eight hours to give me your answer then the deal is off the table.'

'I've already given you my answer!'

'Forty-eight hours…' he repeated, his eyes roving over her flushed face and her defiant yet tellingly shaken expression. 'And let's just wait and see if your answer remains the same after you've…thought things through.'

CHAPTER FIVE

BETH TELEPHONED THAT evening. She could barely contain her excitement. She might be able to hang on to the shelter!

'What do you mean?' Chase asked tentatively. She had spent the past few hours unable to get down to work. Alessandro's offer kept playing in her head over and over again, like a tape recording on a loop. She had stalked out of his house, her head held high, and he had made no attempt to stop her. She thought that that, in itself, displayed a level of arrogance that should really have had her turning her back on him for ever. She loathed arrogance.

Unfortunately, along with her determination not to be browbeaten into making a pact with the devil, there lurked the uncomfortable awareness that, devil or not, he roused something in her she didn't want but couldn't resist. He had kissed her and her whole world had felt as though it had been tilted on its side. It was the same something that had been there eight years ago; the same something that had made her behave in a way she had known she shouldn't. Sexual attraction: he had put his finger on it. Sexual attraction and more…

'I had a call from Mr Moretti.'

'Ah…' She drifted over to the sofa and sat down.

'He's a lot more compassionate than I originally gave him credit for. You know, when this whole business started, well, I just thought of him as a human bulldozer, not caring what or who got in his way.'

Chase smirked. 'What did he say?'

'That he's spoken to you and you've both come up with a plan to secure the future of the shelter; you're both trying to iron out the creases. Chase, my dear, I can't tell you how overjoyed I would be if this worked out. I've been dreading telling the girls that they'll have to go, plus the waiting list is so long of people who need us. Not to mention the seaside idea. Never could quite see myself retiring by the coast and having coffee mornings with all the other retirees.'

'I'm sure there's more to life by the coast than coffee mornings.' Her mind was in a whirl. She was also incensed. So much for the forty-eight hours after which her decision would be final! How could she have been foolish enough to believe that Alessandro wouldn't exert influence over a decision he wanted? 'Lots of people go down there to…er…sail…' she said vaguely.

'Can't think of anything worse. Drive me mad!'

'Did he mention what this idea of…ours happens to be?' Chase prodded gently.

'Not a word!' Beth hooted. 'Said it was something he wanted kept up his sleeve. Probably to do with tax!'

'Sorry?'

'Well, don't these awfully rich people enjoy tax breaks by giving money to charity? We *are* a registered charity…'

Chase sighed and decided to lay off the details of any such scheme. Despite a sharp brain and her degree in engineering, Beth's interest in all things financial was sketchy at best.

'Sometimes,' she said, noncommittal.

'At any rate, it all sounds very promising. I know what you're going to say, my dear! Don't count your chickens… But I get a good feeling from that young man. Did the minute I met him. Showed a real interest in everything we do here at the shelter.'

Alternatively, Chase thought, the man was a skilled actor with a golden tongue. Take your pick.

She spent another twenty minutes on the line as Beth waxed lyrical about Alessandro, and as soon as her friend was off the phone she hunted down the business card he had given her and telephoned him on his mobile.

'Well, that was a low trick!' was the first thing she said the minute she heard his voice on the other end.

At a little after nine, Alessandro had just finished wrapping up a two-hour conference call and was about to leave the office, which was deserted aside from him. In the act of reaching for his jacket, he flung it down on the leather sofa instead and relaxed to take her call. 'So Beth called you,' he drawled without an ounce of shame. 'I thought she might. She certainly was over the moon when I spoke to her. Charming woman.'

'You're a low-down, sneaky rat!'

Alessandro grinned. Whatever Chase's downsides, she was by far and away the most outspoken, feisty woman he had ever met in his entire life. It would probably be a tiresome trait in the long run, but just for the moment it was certainly invigorating.

'Now, now, now…is that any way to speak to your friend's knight in shining armour?'

Chase detected the wicked grin in his voice and gritted her teeth in frustration. 'What did you tell her?'

'Long conversation. I'll fill you in when we next meet.'

'How could you?'

'How could I what? Make that delightful woman one very happy lady?'

'Try and twist my arm into accepting your…your… No, I take that back; I understand perfectly how you did that!'

'It's comforting to know that you can read me like a

book. That way, there will be no mixed messages between us. Now, why don't you carry on working and I'll call you in the morning?'

'I haven't been able to do a scrap of work today!'

'Too busy thinking about me?'

Chase made an inarticulate sound of pure frustration and racked her brains for a clever riposte.

'Well, why don't you get some well-deserved beauty sleep and we'll talk in the morning…or later, if you'd like. After all, your forty-eight hour deadline won't yet be up. Don't worry. I'll be in touch.'

She was left clutching the phone which had gone dead because he had hung up on her. He'd barely heard her out! She felt that there was a lot more anger to be expressed. Unfortunately, without an adversary at which to direct her attack, she was left simmering and fuming on her own as she flounced down in front of the television, having abandoned all attempts at reviewing her caseload.

She was barely aware of what she was watching. It appeared to be a crime drama with an awful lot of victims and an extremely elusive murderer. She had fully zoned out of the story line when, at a little after ten, she heard the insistent buzz of the doorbell and was jerked into instant red alert.

Alessandro.

Surely he wouldn't have the cheek to show up at this hour at her house?

Of course he wouldn't. Why would a shark bother to stalk a minnow when it knew full well that the minnow would swim into its gaping jaw of its own free will?

Much more likely that it was Beth; as she slipped on her bedroom slippers and padded out to the front door, she was already trying to work out what she might say to begin killing her friend's already full-blown optimism.

She pulled open the door to Alessandro and her mouth fell open in surprise.

'Rule one,' he said, strolling past her to take up residence in the sitting room before she had had a chance to marshal her thoughts into order. 'When living in London, never open the door unless you know who's going to be standing on your doorstep.' He turned towards her, which instantly made her feel like a guest in her own home. 'I could have been anyone.'

'And, unfortunately for me, you're not!' She folded her arms and looked at him with gimlet-eyed stoniness. 'What are you doing here?'

'You said that you were finding it impossible to get down to work because you were thinking of me, so I thought I'd drop by.'

'I never said any such thing!' He was not in work clothes but in a pair of black jeans and a grey polo-necked shirt. He looked drop-dead gorgeous, which did nothing for her composure, because she felt far from drop-dead anything in her tatty old jogging bottoms and a tee-shirt that had lost its shape in the wash years ago. She also wasn't wearing a bra and she was conscious of her nipples poking against the cotton of the tee-shirt.

'I must have misunderstood. My apologies. But I'm here now, so maybe you could offer me a cup of coffee? Nothing stronger. I'm driving.'

'I wasn't about to offer you anything!'

'Don't you want to let off steam? You were breathing brimstone and fire down the line less than an hour ago.'

'Because you went behind my back and led Beth to believe that you were going to save her shelter—worse, led her to believe that the decision lies with *me*!'

'Oh, but it does, doesn't it?' He stared at her with a mixture of cool certainty and mild surprise that she should question the obvious.

'What on earth did you tell her?'

'That you and I were working on a plan to see whether the place could be saved and money invested.'

'Because you're such a good guy, right?'

'Let's not go down the tortuous route of moral ethics, Chase. However non-existent you think mine are, you're not exactly in a position to point fingers.'

Chase chewed her lip and glared impotently at him. 'I'll make you some coffee.' She shrugged and turned away. He was here now, in her house, smug and self-satisfied at the awkward position into which he had shoved her; sooner or later they would have to talk, so why not make it sooner? She couldn't see herself getting to sleep in a hurry.

She returned with two mugs of coffee to find him ensconced in one of the deep chairs, the very picture of a man totally relaxed in his surroundings.

'You gave me your word that I would have forty-eight hours.'

'And nothing's changed on that front,' Alessandro said smoothly. 'You still do. I've just thrown an extra something into the mix.'

'And that wasn't fair.'

'Between us, the gloves are off. You're as scheming as I am, so don't even bother to try and play the wounded party with me.' He had not been able to get her out of his head and, the more he thought about her, the more urgent his need to have her became. The sooner he had her, sated this voracious lust, the faster he would be rid of her. He couldn't wait.

Nudging the back of his mind was the uncomfortable truth that he was not a vengeful man by nature, that this sort of revenge was born from emotions which he had handed over to her eight years ago only to find them thrown back in his face. She had shown him his vulnerability and the force of his reactions now lay in that one, unmentioned reality. It was something he could hardly stand to admit even to himself and it lay there, buried like a pernicious weed, even when he had told himself over the years that he had had a narrow escape; that getting involved with a woman such as she had turned out to be would have been an unmitigated disaster.

'You think you know me,' Chase muttered bitterly, and Alessandro narrowed his eyes to look at her.

'By which you mean… Tell me.'

'Nothing,' she said in a harried undertone. 'This is an impossible situation.'

'No, it's not. It's the sound of the wheel turning full circle.'

'You don't like me, you don't respect me, so why on earth would you want to sleep with me? You must be able to snap your fingers and have a thousand women standing to attention and saluting. Why bother with the one who doesn't want to fall in line?'

Chase projected into the future. So she turned him down and the shelter became a shopping mall with her friend retreating to the seaside, where she would live out the rest of her days, bored, grumbling and dissatisfied. Furthermore, what would happen to their friendship? Alessandro had put her in an invidious position, for would her friend ever forgive her for being the one who failed to 'iron out the crease' that would have enabled her to hang on to what she loved?

She would never be able to tell Beth what that particular crease was and eventually the wonderful friendship they had would wither and die under the weight of Beth's misunderstanding and simmering resentment. How could it not?

'I've always considered myself a man to rise to the challenge,' Alessandro said coolly.

'And I'm your challenge.' There was no point moaning

about the unfairness of fate. He had seriously upped the ante by involving Beth and now she had to step up to the plate one way or another. He might well consider himself a guy who couldn't resist a challenge, but when had *she* ever been the sort of woman to back down? Her days of doing that had been put behind her.

And he talked about unfinished business… Wasn't it the same for her? Over the years, through everything that had happened, hadn't he been the burr under her skin? Hadn't she had broken nights dreaming of him? Hadn't she replayed scenarios in her head during which what they had had came to fruition?

More to the point, hadn't all those scenarios sprung back into instant life the second she had laid eyes on him again? Common sense had wrestled with what she considered her stupid weakness, because he was as out of bounds now as he had ever been, despite the fact that Shaun was no longer on the scene. But common sense was failing to win the battle. She knew she looked at him, wondered…

'Are you going to tell me that I'm not yours?' Alessandro asked softly. Two adults, he thought, who wanted each other and this time no hidden obstacle lurking in the way. On top of that, so much for her to get out of it. So where was the problem? He had never had the slightest curiosity to plumb the hidden depths of any woman, yet now he had a sudden, urgent desire to reach into her head and discover what was going on behind that beautiful, enigmatic facade. The thrill of the unexplored was heady and erotic and it took a surprising amount of will power to remain where he was, holding on to silence as a weapon of persuasion.

'It feels…odd. Just not right.'

'But you can't deny that what I'm saying makes sense. If we cut through all the redundant emotion, if we leave bitterness and the past aside, don't we still fancy the hell out of one another?'

Chase thought of his hands on her body, touching her. She had stayed far away from the opposite sex over the past eight years. Offers had been plentiful, some of them horribly insistent, but there was no way she was going to get involved with any man ever again.

So here she was, nearing thirty, unattached, with barely any social life to speak of. Wasn't it time for her to rejoin the human race? And wouldn't she be able to do that once, as he had put it, business between them was finally finished? If she were brutally honest with herself, hadn't Alessandro been as much a reason for where she was now with her life, as Shaun had been? He had had such a dramatic hold on her all those years ago and the way things had ended between them had scarred her to the extent that she had just simply withdrawn.

'It just feels so…cold and detached. So businesslike.' She rubbed her lightly perspiring hands along the soft cotton of her jogging pants.

'You're looking for flowers and chocolates and courtship?' His mouth curled into a cynical smile. 'I believe I fell into that trap once before. I don't repeat my mistakes twice.'

Chase thought she could detect the rapid beating of her heart as he stared at her broodingly. She felt as though she had one foot raised over the edge of a precipice as she made her mind up as to whether to jump or not. Yet, she knew that that was a fallacy. She was older, wiser and tougher and, if this felt like a business arrangement, then it had to be said that business arrangements came with definite upsides. For starters, she would know all the parameters. She would not be hurt. She would be taking from him just as he would be taking from her and, when they walked away from each other, she would be freed from the strange half-emptiness of regret that had been her companion for the past eight years.

It was a tantalising thought.

As though she had opened a door to a gremlin, she was suddenly released from the constraints of having to fight the attraction that had been gnawing away at her. She *imagined*...and the images were so vivid that she felt faint.

'I can't think of anything I would want less than a courtship,' she informed him with as much cool detachment as she could muster. Certainly not flowers or chocolate. He had given her those once before. He must have realised, in the aftermath of her dumping him, that those tokens had hit the bin before she had had time to make it back to her flat. Thank goodness she had bluntly refused to accept anything else. At least he would never be able to add 'gold-digger' to all the other bitter insults he had heaped on her.

Watching her closely, Alessandro knew that he had won. She was going to be his. And yet, instead of the satisfaction of accomplishment, he was irked by the notion that she didn't want a courtship because she had already had a courtship from the one guy who had really counted in her life.

Who gave a damn about the ex-husband? The bald fact was that the man was no longer around and the one woman who had eluded him was going to be his. He was not now, and never would be, in competition with a ghost. When he was through with her, he would discard her and she could return to the photo albums she had stashed in a drawer somewhere. He didn't care. He would have got the one and only thing he wanted from her and for which, essentially, he was prepared to pay a high price, bearing in mind all the money that would need pumping into that shelter if it was to achieve habitable status.

'Is that because you've decided to limit yourself to one and that role was filled by your dearest, departed ex—or because you've had so many in the intervening years that you're sick of them?'

'I've been so busy in the past few years that I haven't had time for…for any kind of relationship.' How strange it felt to be sharing this kind of confidential information! Over time, she had become defined by her need for privacy. She knew that most of her colleagues her age thought she was weird. She knew they thought that, with her looks, she should be putting herself out there instead of working all the hours God made before scuttling off to a house to which none of them had ever been invited. She didn't care, and she had become so accustomed to self-containment that she now looked at Alessandro, wide-eyed, startled by her outburst.

'You mean…?' Curiosity kicked in with cursed force.

'There's actually nothing out of the ordinary about that. Relationships require time and I haven't had a lot of that while I've been trying to climb up the career ladder.' Chase knew how she sounded: tough, hard, cold. This wasn't the person she had ever set out to be but she wasn't going to apologise for the fact that her life hadn't been a round of parties, late nights and sex with random men.

'So ever since your husband died…?' he encouraged.

Chase tilted her chin defensively. 'I know how it must sound to someone like you.'

'Someone like me?'

'I expect you have an active sexual life. Lots of women. You're rich, you're good-looking, you're self-assured. You wouldn't have a clue how I could…hold off on relationships for quite a long time.'

'I managed it eight years ago. With you.' He shook his head, impatient with himself. And he did, actually, understand. Grief and mourning could do all sorts of things and have all manner of consequences. That said…

'It's not healthy,' he said brusquely.

Chase reddened. 'I haven't asked for your opinion,' she

said defensively. 'And the only reason I'm telling you this is because you might want to have a rethink.'

'Not following you.'

'I'm a little rusty in that particular area.' She gave a brittle, nonchalant laugh, but inwardly every part of her felt exposed, vulnerable and uncertain. What on earth was she doing? She wasn't like the women she imagined him being drawn to; she lacked the finesse and the experience. Did she want to risk the humiliation of having him look at her with amusement and disappointment just because she needed to know what she had missed all those years ago? Because, sure, the shelter would be a happy bonus, but she was already yielding for reasons that were far more complex than the desire to save her friend's shelter. Shelter or no shelter, she would never have allowed herself to be manipulated into doing something she didn't want to do.

Alessandro frowned. He had been quick to assert that his proposal was a non-negotiable arrangement designed to assuage the inconvenient need he had to sleep with her and thereby get her out of his system. He had been even quicker to inform her that he would not be investing it with any bells and whistles. It would be sex, no more or less. Yet, he found that he didn't care for the cool approach she was taking. Hell, she was still sitting a million miles away from him!

'I'll cope. Does that mean that you've made your mind up?'

'Perhaps you're right. Perhaps I've been curious. Maybe we do need to…eh…take what we have a step further.' Her heart was beating like a drum. 'But if I accept,' she continued firmly, because it was important for him to know that she wasn't making a decision based on blackmail or unfair persuasion, 'it's not to do with the shelter. Much as I love Beth, I would never do something I didn't want to because of her.'

'Right now, the only thing that matters is that we're going to be lovers.' He gave her a slashing, sexy smile and patted the space next to him on the sofa. 'So why don't you come and sit next to me and we can continue *bonding* with a little less physical distance between us?'

Chase thought she could actually hear her own painful breathing. Fear and apprehension at touching him, being close to him, warred with unbridled excitement. She had stepped off the side of the precipice and she had no idea what she had let herself in for but it was an adventure she needed to have. It was a situation over which she could only hope to exercise control and, for someone who had constructed walls of control all around her, it was a daunting prospect. But she had done daunting before. Many, many times. She could handle daunting.

'How long do you think this will take?'

'Come again?' Alessandro had never had to fight this hard for anyone. Sexual attraction had proved stronger than his very justifiable bitterness and dislike. He had had to swallow a lot and yet, having done that, having got her to the place he wanted, surely the going should get less tough?

'How long do you think it will take before we get past this…thing? A night? A couple of days?'

'How the hell should I know?' Alessandro raked his fingers through his hair and frowned at her. 'And why are we talking about timelines, anyway? All I want to do right now is touch you, so why don't we dispense with the conversation and get down to business?' He sprawled back, arms extended on the back of the sofa, legs loose and open.

He was the very essence of man at his most physical, Chase thought with a shiver, utterly and beautifully masculine; she licked her lips cautiously. She wanted this so badly. It felt as though it was something she had never stopped wanting. She tentatively closed the distance between them to sit like a wooden doll next to him.

'I feel I should tell you,' she whispered as Alessandro lazily removed one arm from the back of the sofa to trail it along her neck.

'You talk a lot,' he growled and then, almost from nowhere, plucked from thin air, 'You always did. As though you had too many words inside you that needed to get out.' He laughed softly, caught unaware by the memory. 'Do you remember the way you would mention a case file and then force me to have an opinion so that you could practise shooting it down in flames?'

Hell, what was he going on about? He angled his body round and pulled her towards him and it was like the promise of heaven. The undiluted thrill of having her in his arms was incomparable and he urgently sought her mouth, plundering it while his hands moved down to circle her waist. His erection was steel-hard and painful. More than anything else, he wanted to rip down those unattractive jogging bottoms, pull aside her panties and then just thrust into her, hard and fast, until he got explosive relief. There would be time enough to do the whole gentle foreplay stuff later.

Chase could feel the raw energy emanating from him in waves but that soft laugh, that nostalgic memory he had laid out bare for her without really thinking, was strangely seductive, strangely relaxing. Fingers that had been curled into his polo shirt suddenly splayed against his chest and she struggled back from him.

'Wait…'

'I'm not sure I can.' But he reluctantly drew back, his breathing ragged and uneven. She was stripped of her tough, outer shell, the consummate lawyer and assertive career woman. He glimpsed a uniquely feminine vulnerability that startled him, because she was the last woman on the planet he would ever have labelled *'vulnerable'*.

Once upon a time, sure, but then once upon a time he'd been an idiot.

'I'm not into playing games,' he drawled just in case she got it into her head that she could string him along for a second time. 'And, just in case you think that you might be able to pull off any "one step forward, two steps back" tactic, then forget it. This time round, you're dealing with a different person, Chase. My levels of tolerance when it comes to you are non-existent.'

'I know they are!' Whatever the backdrop to what they had had eight years ago, it all seemed so innocent now in retrospect. 'It's just…'

'Just *what*, Chase?'

'Never mind.' She wasn't looking for sweet nothings whispered in her ear nor was she looking for any shows of affection. She told herself that she was perfectly comfortable with an 'arrangement', yet as she reached to hook her fingers under the tee-shirt to pull it over her head, she knew that she was breathing too quickly, close to freezing up.

'Oh for goodness' sake,' Alessandro groaned and caught her hands in his. 'Why tell me that this is what you want if you have to squeeze your eyes tightly shut and give every impression of a woman who has to grin and bear it?'

'I *do* want it,' Chase insisted but she could hear the give-away wavering in her voice and she hated it.

'Then what's the problem?' He took in the hectic flush in her cheeks. What was going on here? Shouldn't this be straightforward—two consenting adults getting something out of their system? 'Tell me.'

'You're not really interested.'

'Let me be the one who decides that.' He nuzzled her ear and smiled as she quivered, because it tickled.

'I'm… I've…' She took a deep, steadying breath. 'I've never really been into sex,' she said in a rush. 'I know you can't bear me, and your tolerance levels are low, but I can't just fall on this sofa with you and have wild sex.'

'Never really been into sex?' Alessandro's voice held accusatory disbelief. 'You were a married woman,' he pointed out with ruthless directness. 'Married at what age—eighteen? Younger? Are you telling me that you were a gymslip wife who didn't enjoy sleeping with her husband?'

'I don't want to talk about Shaun,' Chase said quickly. *Or,* she mentally tacked on, *anything to do with my past, the past you think you know but don't.*

Alessandro looked at her in silence for a long time. She was flustered as hell but trying hard to put on a show of strength and assertiveness. Did he need all of this? It was just sex and, yet again, that surge of curiosity that was more insistent than the cold logic he wanted to impose. 'Why don't you want to talk about him?'

'Because…there's no point. I'll just say that things are never what you think they are.' Too much information. 'But it's been a long time for me…' she concluded hurriedly.

'You just want me to take it slowly, do you?'

Chase nodded.

'In that case, what about a show of good faith?' He shot her a slow smile. 'Taking it slow is one thing,' he murmured, playing with a strand of her hair whilst he tried to halt his runaway mind, which wanted to ask her what she had meant by her enigmatic remark about things never being what you thought they were. 'A standstill pace, on the other hand, just won't do. So why don't we both get naked and see what happens next?' He watched her carefully, wanting her more than anything, prepared to do the complex if that was what it took. 'If you're not comfortable down here, then you could always give me a tour of upstairs and we can end up in your bedroom. How does that sound?'

Chase nodded. 'You might be disappointed at what you see.' She tried to make her voice as normal as possible but her pulse was racing as they quietly padded upstairs. 'The whole of my upstairs could probably fit into your downstairs cloakroom.'

He wanted a show of good faith and she couldn't blame him. She pushed open the doors to the small spare room, with its single futon, the desk at which she was accustomed to working until late into the night and the bathroom which was large and airy given the size of the house. They ended up in her bedroom.

Alessandro stood in the doorway and looked. The walls were a subdued cream but the four-poster bed was dressed and all romance. The prints on the walls were landscapes of deserted beaches. The dressing table, like the wardrobe, was old, doubtless bought at auction. He thought that he might be the first guy to step foot in this room and it gave him an unbelievable kick. Every single woman he had ever known had been keen to show him their bedrooms and the beds which promised inventive entertainment for as long as he wanted. Mood lighting had usually been a dominant theme. When he took in Chase's wary expression, he could see ambivalence there.

'Your sanctuary.'

'Not any longer. You're in it.'

'By invitation.' His hand reached to the button on his trousers, but first he removed the shirt in one easy movement.

Chase practically fainted. He was the stuff daydreams were made of and she had had enough of those over the years. His body was burnished gold and honed to perfection. When he moved, she could detect the ripple of muscle under skin. Her breathing picked up pace and her mouth went dry. Under her top, her bare breasts tingled, and she had the heady feeling that she wanted them touched, that she wanted her nipples played with.

'Your turn…' He liked the way her eyes skittered across his body as if helplessly drawn to stare at him. He remembered the way that used to do crazy things to him once and was uneasily aware that that should have changed—so why hadn't it? He found that he was holding his breath as her tee-shirt slowly rode up her belly, exposing her pale skin a slither at a time. She wasn't doing this because of undue pressure, yet there was an erotic hesitancy about her movements. The wealth of all her complexities crashed over him like a wave from which he had to fight to surface, to bring himself back in the moment.

He was a randy teenager all over again as he looked at her breasts, heavy and sexy and everything he had imagined. More. Her breasts were bigger than he had thought, tipped with perfect rosy-pink discs. She possessed a body that should never be constrained by a starchy lawyer's outfit. Her proportions were all feminine curves: bountiful breasts, a narrow waist and proper hips that swelled tantalisingly under the dreary track pants. He wanted nothing more than to stride over to her and feel her nakedness pressed against him.

With some sixth sense, though, he was aware of her skittishness. He didn't get it, but he could feel it. Any sudden moves and he got the feeling that she would take flight, even though she obviously wasn't embarrassed about her body, wasn't trying to be coy and hide her breasts behind her hands. He kept his eyes on her face as he removed his trousers and flung them to one side, still looking at her.

Chase felt her skin tighten at the glaring evidence of his arousal. His dark boxers could hardly contain it. She shakily reached to the elasticised waist of her joggers and stilled as he moved towards her.

'You look as though you want to run away,' he murmured. He swallowed hard because the tips of her breasts were almost brushing his chest and his hands itched to feel the weight of them. 'Believe it or not, this is taking it slow by my standards.'

'I believe you,' Chase said huskily. She touched his chest with one finger and felt his soft moan.

'Come to bed.' He stepped away from her. 'I'm not sure how long the slow plan can carry on for.'

When he turned his back to her, Chase knew that he was trying to hold himself back. She felt giddy with power. It was a wonderfully novel sensation and it afforded her a layer of strength she hadn't known she possessed. With Shaun, it had never been like this, never, not even in the very beginning. But she didn't want to think about her ex-husband. That was one very fast and very sure route to instant depression.

She slipped out of the jogging bottoms; his back was still turned when she crept into bed and under the covers.

'Now…' He wasn't used to taking sex slowly. He had never had to pace himself. He failed to consider that pacing himself with a woman for whom he harboured nothing more than a desire to even the score made no sense. 'Tell me…' he flipped onto his side so that they were lying under the covers, front to front, their bodies not touching but both of them vitally aware of their nudity under the duvet '…about the prints on your walls. And the four-poster bed…'

CHAPTER SIX

IF THERE WERE prizes for holding a man's interest, then Alessandro thought that Chase would be in line for all of them. He had planned on a straightforward conquest, aided and abetted by the trump card of saving the shelter. He would take her and, by taking her, he would rid himself of the allure of the inaccessible—which was the position to which she seemed to have been elevated over the years, apparently without him even having noticed. For him, the accessible had always had a short-lived appeal, especially when the quarry in question came with a truckload of dubious cargo.

And she had played him at his own game, had not been browbeaten but had laid her cards on the table. But then that hesitancy, that tentative admission that sex wasn't her thing… She had lain in his arms but he could feel her tension and he had backed off, even though his body had been on fire for her.

The rapacious, lying, deceitful, manipulative woman had shown a shrinking violet side to her that had got under his skin. Since when had he become the sort of man who was content to hold off, especially in a situation like this, with a woman scarcely worth his time and attention? He had held off with her once and look at where that had got him! But had he done what he should have done? Had he sneered at her attempts to play the shy maiden and ploughed forward? Hell, no! He had lain with her in his arms like the virgin she most certainly was not, had *talked*, and then he had left to return to his apartment and a freezing-cold shower.

Then he had gone abroad for two days, giving himself time to figure out why he was behaving so out of character and giving her time to wise up to the fact that what they had was a deal—and one he intended to cash, because her time limit for playing shy had been used up. He had returned late last night with two flights to Italy booked and the decidedly uncomfortable realisation that there might just be a need to shift gears slightly—to woo her, despite everything he had said about what they had not being a courtship. Somewhere along the line the whole 'time limit' speech had been shelved.

He just knew that when she came to him she would come of her own volition. She would jettison whatever the hell it was that was holding her back. In the space of a heartbeat, it had become a matter of pride—actually in the space of time it had taken for the notion of a break in Italy to take root, which had been fairly instantaneous.

If she was holding back because she hadn't managed to put the premature death of her husband behind her, then she needed to move on from that place and come to him willingly. There was no way he was going to sleep with any woman unless her thoughts were focused one hundred per cent on him and, if it took some seduction to get her to that place, then he would play along with it. The end result would be the same, wouldn't it? And he was an 'end result' kind of guy.

He had phoned her from abroad and announced the whole Italy idea with far more conviction than he had been feeling at the time, but she had taken little persuading as it turned out in the end. She was due some time off and she would take it. A little more enthusiasm would have been appreciated but he had met his match in her. She hadn't pandered to him eight years ago and she wasn't going to pander to him now, even though she knew him for the billionaire that he was.

Now, standing in front of the check-in desk at Heathrow surrounded by crowds, he scowled as he felt himself inevitably harden at the tantalising prospect of having her; of touching that flawless body; of sinking against those breasts, feeling them against his chest, against the palms of his big hands, pushing into his mouth. He had once lost his head over a mirage and now he would take what he felt was his due, take the promised fruit and kill the bitterness inside him that made such an unwelcome companion.

Through the crowds he spotted her weaving and looking around for him and he gave her a brief wave.

'You're ten minutes late. You should have let my driver collect you instead of coming by public transport.'

Chase looked up at his frowning face and was tempted to snap because, however much she wore her hard-won independence like a badge of honour, he obviously had a Neanderthal approach to women in general. But she bit back the retort because she could remember the way he had always taken command when she had known him: paying for whatever they had before she could offer to go halves; impatient with second-rate service; intolerant of anyone in his lectures who'd failed to try.

'I told you. I had some work to finish before I left.' Left for a week in the sun. She had no idea where that idea of Alessandro's had sprung from. She had fought against going, because she was all too aware that their relationship was destined to crash and burn, and the last thing she needed was a plethora of memories she would later have to work out of her system, but he had been insistent. Maybe being out of the country would infuse this weird closure of theirs with an unreality that would be easy to box away.

Italy, he had told her, was his home and, hell, why not. It was a nice time of year over there and he had just closed a massive deal. She could see his house. His casual tone of voice down the end of the line had told her that it wasn't a big deal. He would be going over there himself, she figured, with her or without her, but he would take her along because, as far as he was concerned, she had yet to fulfil her side of the bargain. Lying naked in his arms, tense as a plank of wood, didn't count.

Had they had sex, she was sure that he would not have suggested the Italy trip. Revenge lay behind his motivation and revenge was an emotion that could be sated very quickly. Certainly, a week of her would be enough. Did she deserve that? Maybe she did, in his eyes, and she would never disabuse him of the complicated story behind her lies because that would open up a whole new can of worms far worse than the one she was dealing with.

'Isn't that the old hoary line used by men?' Alessandro queried, moving towards the check-in girl at the first class desk. It occurred to him that he would have quite enjoyed having her at his beck and call and put that down to a caveman instinct he'd never known he possessed. Or maybe he only possessed it when the chase was still on, and only with her because she hadn't followed the pattern of the women he slept with.

'You're very chauvinistic, Alessandro. Women who have careers can't just jettison them the second something better comes along. As it is, I'll have a mountain of work to get down to when I get back. I shouldn't really be here at all, even if I *am* due time off.'

'Are you telling me that being with me is more compelling than your career?'

'I'm not saying anything of the sort!'

'You work too hard.'

'How else am I expected to get on?'

'What are you expecting to *get on* to?' They had checked in and were now heading through Passport Control, towards the first class lounge. Years ago he had considered the possibility of a private jet, if only to cut down on the inconvenience of a bustling airport, but had ditched the idea, because who needed to be responsible for such a vast personal carbon footprint when it could be avoided? Shame, though, because, had he had one, he could have introduced her to some creative ways of passing time twenty thousand miles up without an audience of prying eyes.

'I'd like to head up my own pro bono department. Maybe even branch out on my own and concentrate on that area. Bring in a few other employees…who knows?'

'And what about another prance up the aisle? Is that up there on the agenda? Surely your parents would want to hear the patter of little feet when you visit them in Australia? Or do visits to Australia get in the way of your career?'

Chase temporarily froze. The passing lie was not one on which she wanted to dwell. She wanted no reminders of her non-existent family. She knew that the last thing he would want to discuss would be her ex or her past treachery. His only goal was to get her into bed; her only goal was to put this murky, tangled, haunting past to rest. He was motivated by revenge, she by a need for closure. It was a straightforward situation. She needed no reminders of white lies that had been told and could not now be un-told.

How would he react were he to know that, not only had she once lied to him about her marital status, not only had she dumped him in a way that now made her cringe with guilt and shame even though she knew that it just couldn't have been helped at the time, but that her entire past was as substantial as gossamer?

'Australia is a long way away…' she muttered vaguely.

'Yes. I know. I've been there. You've never told me which part of Australia they live in. It's a big place.'

'You wouldn't have heard of it.' She could feel beads of perspiration break out all over her body. 'It's just a small town on the outskirts of…um…Melbourne. Look, I really don't want to talk about this. Discussing personal issues isn't what we're about, is it?' Never had she realised how being trapped in a lie could prove as painful as walking on a bed of burning coals.

'No,' Alessandro said shortly. 'It's not.' He looked at her blank eyes and tight smile and felt a surge of rage that the thing most women gave naturally to him—the desperate openness which they always seemed to hope could suck him into something permanent and committal—was the one thing Chase steadfastly refused to give. It angered him that he was even going down the road of quizzing her because it reflected a series of inner challenges that he knew were inappropriate. The challenge to get her into bed so that he could assuage the treachery he felt had been done to him had been replaced by the challenge to get her into bed willingly and *hot for him*; the challenge to wipe her ex out of her head when they finally had sex, the challenge to get into her head, to know what made her tick.

Where the hell did it end? Did he need her to remind him that the rules of the game precluded certain things?

'Call it making polite conversation,' he offered with cool politeness.

'I overreacted. It's just that…'

'No need to explain yourself. I'm basically not interested in your past. Like I said, small talk…'

Chase was silenced. Of course he was basically not interested in her past. He was basically not interested in *her*. He was utterly focused on one thing and one thing only. She nodded, nonchalantly indicating that she understood, that she shared the same sentiment.

When he began telling her about some of the complex legalities of the deal he had just pulled off, she let herself slide smoothly into career-woman mode, and then the conversation flowed faultlessly onto the subject of Beth and the shelter. It was a happy story and Chase felt herself once again relax. This was an odd situation but she could handle it, just as long as she didn't start feeling angst over stuff, just as long as she maintained the composed exterior that was so much part and parcel of her personality. She couldn't let herself forget that she wanted this as much as he did. They both had their demons to put to rest.

They landed at Cristoforo Colombo Airport at Genova Sestri to a brilliant day. The wall-to-wall blue skies, which had no longer been in evidence in London after their brief appearance, were here in full force. As soon as they stepped into the waiting limo, she could feel a heady holiday spirit fill her.

'It's been ages since I've been away,' she confided as she settled back to watch the stunning scenery gallop past from the back of the car. 'In fact…' she turned to him '…my only trip abroad in the past few years has been a snatched week at a spa resort in Greece.'

'In that case, I shall make it my mission to see that you enjoy every second of my country…when and if we have the time; bed can be remarkably compulsive with the right companion in it.' His dark eyes roved over her face, encompassing her luscious body, enjoying the delicate bloom of colour that tinged her cheeks.

This holiday would put an end to the game playing which he had sworn he wouldn't tolerate, yet had ended up indulging that one night which should have seen this uncontrollable passion slayed. As she had pointed out in a timely reminder, this wasn't about getting to know one another, this was about sex. Getting to know one another had been a pointless game which he had mistakenly played a long time ago, little knowing that he had been the only participant.

This time round, there'd be no more messing around and taking things at a snail's pace. He would move only as slowly as he felt necessary to get her where he wanted her—which was out of his system so that he could return to normality.

Vaguely annoyed at the contrary drift of his thoughts, he was aware of telling her about the Italian Riviera, on autopilot, pointing out the grandeur of the mountainous landscape in such close and unusual proximity to the sea, giving her a little bit of history about the place. His voice warmed as he described the vast olive grove plantations stretching across the hills, vast tracts of which had once been owned by his ancestors, only to disappear over the years, mismanaged and sold off in bits and pieces—the last by his parents, who had needed the money in their quest for eternal fun.

'You could always come back here…buy more olive groves. It's so beautiful; I can't see why you would want to live in London.' Not even in her wildest, escapist fantasies could she ever have dreamt up somewhere as beautiful as this. The landscape was bold and dramatic, the colours bright and vibrant. Everywhere was bursting with incredible, Technicolor beauty. Alessandro might have had irresponsible parents but it had to be said that, whatever he had gone through, he had gone through it in some style.

'I have a house here. It's where we're going.'

'But how often do you visit it?'

'As you'll be the first to agree, taking time out gets in the way of a career.'

Chase bristled at the implicit criticism in his remark. It reminded her that what they shared was simply a truce but, behind that truce, there was a lot he just didn't like about her. 'My career is important to me.'

'I've gathered.'

'You say that as though you disapprove of women who work.'

'On the contrary. Some of the highest positions in my company are occupied by women.'

'But you would never actually go out with a woman who had a career...'

Alessandro shot her a sidelong glance. The car was air-conditioned but he had chosen to have the windows opened and the breeze blew through her hair, tossing it across her face in unruly strands. She was no longer the high-powered lawyer with the pristine appearance. She was the girl he had once known and he railed against the pull of memories. 'There's little I find attractive about a woman who puts her career first.'

Chase rolled her eyes and sighed, because the breeze was too balmy and the scenery too exotic for arguing. 'That is because you're a dinosaur.' He had old-fashioned ideas. Years ago she had teased him that that was a backlash from his parents' excesses but she had liked those old-fashioned ideas, never having come across them before.

'And I take it that under normal circumstances you wouldn't choose to go out with a dinosaur? Tell me about your husband.'

'I no longer have a husband,' Chase said shortly, rousing herself from bittersweet memories of their brief, shared dalliance.

'I realise that. What was he like?' He was curious. He found that he wanted to know. This wasn't polite conversation, although the casual tone of his voice gave nothing away.

The last thing Chase wanted to do was to talk about Shaun but she had a sneaking suspicion that, if she backed away from the subject, it would arouse his interest even further. 'We met when we were young. I was only fifteen. Just. We met at the local disco.'

'Cosy. And was it love at first sight?'

'We found that we had a lot in common.'

'Always a good start to a healthy relationship. Even at the ripe old age of fifteen. Just.' He found that he didn't care for the idea of them having a lot in common at whatever the hell age they had happened to meet. Nor had he intended to get wrapped up in pointless conversations about the thug who had been lurking behind the scenes when she had taken him for a ride and played him for a fool.

'So they say,' Chase murmured tonelessly.

'I take it he wasn't sharp enough to make it to university?'

'Shaun was plenty sharp.' She couldn't help the bitterness that had crept into her voice but she kept it at bay. Talking about Shaun would inevitably lead to all sorts of questions about the sort of world she had really come from. Chase found that she had moved on from the fear of him discovering the truth about her and eking out some kind of belated revenge by spilling the beans to her work colleagues. She honestly couldn't see him doing that.

No, what she feared—and she hated herself for this—was to have him walk away in disgust at the lies she had told, at the person she really was and the life she had really led. His pedigree was impeccable and although she knew that they would be the archetypal doomed lovers—in it for the wrong reasons but driven to fulfil their destiny—she still found that she wanted him to believe her to be the sassy, smart lawyer with the perfectly ordinary background when they parted company.

Wasn't that to be expected? What if she bumped into him at a later date? What if he met some of the partners in her law firm and started talking about her? If he knew the truth about her, then wasn't it likely that it would slip out in conversation? And, even if nothing did slip out, surely he would never be able to disguise the contempt in his voice at the mention of her name?

'Sharp as in…?'

She snapped out of her daydreaming to find his eyes narrowed on her. 'Streetwise; sharp as in streetwise.'

'And did your streetwise late husband have a job?' He thought back to the picture she had shown him all those years ago.

'He…worked in transport but he…he lost his job shortly before the accident. I'd bought him that motorbike. I'd been putting aside some money and I wanted to celebrate getting my first promotion…'

'So you celebrated by buying him a motorbike. Shouldn't *he* have been the one doing the buying to congratulate you? Or am I just thinking like a dinosaur again?'

'Alessandro, please, let's move on from this. I honestly don't want to talk about Shaun. Tell me more about here. It's amazing to think that there can be snow on mountaintops that are just a short distance from the Med…'

Alessandro heard the soft plea in her voice. 'Why did you give me a second look if you were so clearly head over heels in love with your husband?'

'I…I'm sorry. I made a mistake.'

'Which doesn't answer my question.' He raked his hand impatiently though his hair and sat back with his eyes closed for a few seconds. 'Scrap that. Not sure I could stomach whatever fairy stories you decide to come out with.'

'Alessandro…'

He inclined his head towards her and linked his fingers loosely in his lap. She had the face of an angel, the body of a siren and he was furious with himself for wanting to probe deeper. He pointed to a spot behind her as the car turned left. 'My house.'

Chase turned just in time to glimpse a sand-coloured

mansion rising up from the cliffs, overlooking the placid turquoise sea with a backdrop of woods of chestnut trees. She forgot everything and her mouth dropped open.

'I have two housekeepers who live in, make sure everything is ticking over. Occasionally, it's used by some of my employees, a little bonus if they do well. The promise of an all-expenses-paid long weekend here generates a lot of healthy competition, and it does no harm for the place to get an airing now and again.'

'It's huge. What about family members?'

'Oh, completely off-limits to them. My parents ensured their place in the pecking order as the black sheep of the family and I've inherited their generous legacy. I have little contact with my extended family.

'My parents were both only children, so there are strangely few people who bear a belated grudge towards me. I see a couple of slightly less distant relatives now and again when I'm in Milan; a few more work in some of my associated companies, my way of making amends for my parents' appallingly hedonistic behaviour which was, if all accounts are to be believed, ruinous to both family names.'

He edged towards her and pointed. 'You can't see it, but there's a winding path that leads down to a private cove at the bottom of the cliff face. Excellent bathing. Once upon a time, fishing used to be big here. Not so much any more. Tourism pays better, it would seem. The wealthy find the sight of yachts far more uplifting than the reality of fishing boats.'

'What a shame you don't get here often,' Chase said. When he was like this—charming, informative, his voice as deep and as dark as the most pure, rich, velvety chocolate—she could forget everything. She could lapse back to the past where dangerous, taboo emotions still held a certain innocence, a time when he didn't hate her. 'Don't you sometimes long to have someone to share this with?'

'Oh, but isn't that what I'm doing now?' Alessandro drawled. 'Admittedly, only for a few days, and with a woman who is destined never to return, but it'll do for the moment.'

He reached across, pulling her towards him. 'I've given my loyal housekeepers time off,' he murmured into her hair. 'It's hot here. I thought it might be nice for us to live as naturists for a few days. Why bother with clothes? I want to be able to touch you anywhere…at any time… And you'll discover that my house is perfect for ensuring one hundred per cent privacy. I'll make you thaw, my sweet; on that count, you can trust me…'

Chase was still smarting from the insistent stab of hurt his words had generated. *Destined never to return.*

They approached the sprawling villa through wrought-iron gates which had been flung open, revealing perfectly groomed lawns stretching out on either side of the gravel drive.

'How many people does it take to look after these gardens?' She shouldn't have been, but she was still shocked by the splendour.

'A small army,' Alessandro admitted drily. 'I'm single-handedly trying to do my bit to keep the economy going. There's a very private pool to the side of the house. I have vague memories of my parents throwing some extremely wild parties there.'

'I had no idea the house belonged to them.' Chase turned to look at him and their eyes tangled. Instantly, she could feel her breasts begin to ache in expectation of his caresses. With Shaun, she had become conditioned to viewing sex as something that had to be done. But when she had lain next to Alessandro her body had been fired up in a way that was new and, whilst they hadn't made love, it now thrummed at the prospect of being touched by him. It was a heady, exciting feeling and she was sure that it was all wrapped up in the culmination of what had begun all that time ago, what had never come to fruition.

'It was their pride and joy. The one thing they both hung on to.'

'And you kept it for sentimental reasons?'

'I never do anything for sentimental reasons. It's a good, appreciating asset.'

It was dreamy. If she had been able to conceive of a place like this, she might have been more elaborate in her teenage fantasies about perfect lifestyles instead of just settling for average. Then she decided that it was just as well, because how much more awkward would life have been now had her naïve, happily married parents in their two-up two-down been turned into minor landed gentry living in a small castle?

They were greeted by an elderly housekeeper and her husband who had stayed on to welcome Alessandro, tugging him into the kitchen so that they could show him the freezer full of food that had been prepared and the well-stocked larder. He managed to shoo them away after an hour and they departed wreathed in smiles.

'They've been with me for longer than I care to think. As you know, my parents were firm believers in handing over care of their offspring to hired help,' he told her as he played tour guide, taking her from room to room. He absently thought how many of those little details of his past she had been privy to, courtesy of that small window in his life during which his self-control had gone on holiday.

'I'm treating them to a well-deserved rest in a destination of their choosing, which as it turns out happens to be France, where their eldest is a dentist. I tried to persuade them into somewhere a little further afield but they weren't having it. Mauritius, apparently, is no competition for two hyper grandchildren.'

Chase's heart fluttered. This was how he had managed

to get under her skin. This was why she never wanted to have him learn the truth about her. This was why the thought of what he could do to balance the scales of justice should he want to avenge past wrongs was no longer the only consideration. Underneath his ruthlessly cold exterior were these flashes of genuine thoughtfulness that kept reminding her of why she had risked so much just talking to him eight years ago; that ambushed all her good intentions to keep her distance. Whenever he made her laugh, her defences slipped just a little bit more.

This was a dangerous game because she would end up being hurt. She would end up losing her hard-won self-control. She would end up with someone else having power over her, someone who didn't care about her, who wanted her for all the wrong reasons. Maybe she had already ended up there.

She had walked into this with her eyes wide open but now she felt as though she had walked straight into a trap, having stupidly failed to take account of its power for destruction.

The whole sex thing... Yes, she had wanted it, had *craved* it, but she had been scared because of past experience and he had respected her when she had turned into a block of ice in his arms. That consideration he had shown her, as it turned out, was just something else that had nibbled away at the edges of her defences so that what had once been a fortress, protecting her from the slings and arrows of emotional involvement with the human race, was beginning to resemble a broken down old castle open to all the elements.

She felt exposed in a way she never had in her life before. She felt as she had eight years ago: like a woman *falling in love.*

'You've stopped using rapturous superlatives to describe my house.'

Chase blinked and realised that he was several metres ahead of her because she had stopped dead in her tracks. Her brain had been so wrapped up contemplating the horror of falling for this guy again that it hadn't had any room left to give messages to her legs to keep moving.

'I think I may have run out of them.' She blinked and took in the raw sexuality of the man lounging in front of her with that killer half-smile on his lips.

'Where is this famous pool you've been bragging about?' Her voice was normal but her brain was malfunctioning.

'I never brag.' Again that smile that hurled her back in time. He took her hand to lead her through the house, out to the kitchen and towards the sea-facing side of the house, which took her breath away. 'Except in this one instance.'

He gestured to the open view as though he owned it and then relaxed back to look at her response. He had never given a damn what women thought of his opulent lifestyle and was indifferent to their gasps of awe whenever they stepped foot into his house in London. Yet he rather enjoyed the way her mouth fell open as she stepped out to stand next to him.

The house looked down to the sea that was turquoise and as still as a lake. The garden on this side was just a strip of green, broken by distinctive Italian palm trees and bordered by thick shrubbery. To one side a gate announced the winding stone steps, which Chase imagined led to the cove he had told her about.

This was her dream come true. She had somehow been catapulted into the prints she had hung on her walls. The romance which had not been part of the plan clung to her in a miasma, giving her all sorts of stupid illusions that somehow what they had might be the beginning of something real. It was time to start unravelling that piece of fiction.

'Are you sure it's completely deserted here?' She

squinted against the sun to look up at him, shielding her eyes with one hand.

Alessandro looked down at her. She was in a flimsy sleeveless dress which was far too baggy for his liking but which, on the upside, provided terrific fodder for his imagination. 'As a ghost town. Why?'

'Because I think we should explore that pool area you were bragging to me about… Oh yes, I forgot: you never brag…' Her hand fluttered provocatively to the small top button of the dress. 'It's so warm. I think I might need to strip off, have a dip in that pool of yours, the one—'

'I keep bragging to you about even though I never brag?' He laughed under his breath and felt the bulge in his pants as that part of his body which had been in charge of his brain ever since she had reappeared to smash into his ordered existence rose to immediate attention.

He linked his fingers through hers and began leading her across the lawn, swerving to the side of the house where exuberant flora, lemon trees, shrubs sprouting with brightly coloured flowers and hydrangea enclosed an exquisite infinity pool. The air was aromatic.

'I feel as though I've stepped into a travel brochure.'

Alessandro frowned. A nagging thought occurred to him. Had he seen those prints on the walls and brought her here so that he could deliver her those dreams of sun, sea and sand that had clearly never been realised? Had that been some weird, unconscious motivation behind his invitation to bring her to his house? He irritably swept aside a suspicion with which he was not comfortable.

'You said you were hot…?'

'So I did.' She would have liked to enjoy the scenery a bit more. Well, a lot more. But business was business, wasn't it? The longer this game between them carried on, the deeper her scars would be when they parted company, when he had got what he wanted. She undid the small buttons of the dress and it fell to the ground, pooling at her feet.

Alessandro remained where he was, looking at her with lazy, predatory satisfaction. 'Will this be a full striptease?'

'I want you, Alessandro…' *And I love you. I loved you once and I think it would be very easy to love you again.* She schooled her features to conceal the chaos of her thoughts. 'And I think we've both waited long enough…' She walked towards him, reaching behind her as she did so to unhook her bra, which she tossed onto one of the low, wooden sun loungers, never taking her eyes off his face.

Alessandro found that he could barely control his breathing. The moment was electric. His jaw clenched when she was finally standing in front of him and he had to steel himself against an unruly, premature overreaction as she slipped out of her panties so that she was now completely naked.

'The sun's pretty fierce…' He curved his hand around her waist, idly caressing it and pulling her against him at the same time. 'And you're fair. Any doctor would tell you that you need to lather yourself in sunblock…' He kissed her slowly, tugging her bottom lip with his teeth, gently tasting her mouth, taking his time as their tongues melded, even though it was agony trying to keep his libido in check.

'So what do you want to do about it?' She wrapped her arms around his neck and flung her head back with a sigh as his lips traced a path along the slender column of her neck. She was wet and ready for him. She reached to fumble with the button of his trousers and he stayed her hand.

'One good striptease deserves another,' he murmured in a sexy, shaky undertone that sent her blood pressure skyrocketing. 'But first…'

He sauntered towards what she now saw was a vine-covered pool house and emerged a couple of minutes later with towels and various creams. He dumped them on one of the vacant loungers and she watched, heart beating wildly, as he did what she had done only moments before.

His shirt was tossed to join hers and he kept his eyes on her as he walked slowly towards her. Every inch that brought him closer did crazier things to her nervous system. Her breath caught in her throat as he removed his trousers, then, when she felt that swooning was a real possibility, the final item of clothing joined the rest and he was as naked as she was, his proud, impressive erection proclaiming that he was as turned on as her.

When he was inches away from her, she reached down and firmly circled it with her hand.

'Three days ago you were as tense as a violin string…' He led her towards one of the loungers which was shaded by an overhanging tree and he neatly spread one of the towels on it.

Three days ago, she thought, *I had no idea that my body could feel like this; three days ago it started to come alive. I may have been apprehensive then at what I was feeling but I'm not apprehensive now...*

'I'm not now,' she said huskily.

'Then lie down. I'm going to put sun cream on you and it'll be the best foreplay you've ever experienced…'

CHAPTER SEVEN

'IT MIGHT BE a little cold,' Alessandro murmured. He had to make sure to keep his eyes away from her breasts, away from her flat stomach, away from the soft, downy hair that lightly covered the triangular apex between her thighs. He would save himself. 'I keep the pool house air-conditioned. Lie on your stomach…'

'You honestly don't need to bother with sun lotion. It's perfectly safe here in the shade.'

'Doctor's orders. Safety first is the main thing.' She was on her stomach and very slowly he began to explore every exquisite inch of her body, rubbing the sun cream into her, feeling the silky smoothness of her skin and, with each stroke of his hand on her body, getting more aroused.

He pressed his thumbs gently against each vertebra so that she was moaning softly and melting under his touch. He massaged her neck, then her sides, so that her mind went blank and she sighed and squirmed; then the rounded cheeks of her bottom and the length of her glorious legs which parted temptingly, inviting him to go further, but it was an invitation he wasn't going to take up until he was good and ready.

'This is… I never knew…' It was an inaudible sigh.

'Now, shift over. Lie on your back. We can't let an inch of you go unprotected, can we? I would never forgive my-self if you were to get sunburned.'

Chase, cynical when it came to interpreting everything he said, wondered if he meant that he would never forgive himself should she be out of action while they were over here. Four days in paradise without the sex he had been anticipating wouldn't do, would it?

She nearly laughed hysterically when she thought that four days in paradise with him without sex would still be four days in paradise for her as opposed to a wasted trip.

'And stop frowning. Just relax. Enjoy.' Her face was first and then his long, supple fingers moved to her shoulders. He did his utmost not to look at her breasts, at the large, pink discs that were responding so enthusiastically to what his hands were doing. He was aware, though, that the tips had tightened into hard peaks as she became more and more turned on.

He watched, fascinated, at the slight flare of her nostrils as he began to lavish his attention on her breasts. 'You can't be too careful in this Italian sun…especially for someone with as little experience of hot weather as you.'

'Don't be silly, Alessandro. London gets hot.' Her eyes were shut tightly and her fists clenched in an effort at self-control as he continued to massage her breasts. It felt so good. 'Are you sure we're on our own here?' This as he bent to take one pouting nipple in his mouth and she moaned weakly as he suckled on it while spanning his hand across her rib cage.

'No one else would have permission to see this body,' he broke off to tell her. 'It's for my eyes only.' Then he returned to the matter at hand, moving to pay the same attention to her other nipple.

How long could he keep this up? Straddling her, he nudged her legs apart. Protection for the full thing, naturally. But he couldn't resist the feel of her moistness against him and he rubbed himself along her wet crease, an insistent, rhythmic movement that made her gasp out loud.

'How does this feel, baby?' he asked, his voice raw and unsteady and she whimpered a response that was answer enough. 'I'm not going to come in you. I just need to do this…'

But he had to stop when he knew that a few more seconds and he would push them both over the edge. The anticipation of having full-blown sex with her was filling his mind and sensitising every inch of his body. When she half-raised herself to take him in her hand, he gently pushed her back down. He had to control this. If he didn't, he would come right here, right now and that was something he didn't want to do. This time, he was going to feel the silky smoothness of being deep inside her.

He smoothed the cream over her inner thighs and breathed her in. The sweet, sexy smell of her filled his nostrils and he half-closed his eyes before dipping his head between her legs. The flat of his hands were on her thighs, pushing them apart, and he felt her tiny convulsion as his tongue made contact with her clitoris.

Chase's fingers tangled in his hair. Here, under the shade of a tree, the sun's heat was pleasantly diluted. The breeze was soft and balmy. Half-opening her eyes, she saw his dark head between her thighs and, framing him, the glory of the Italian scenery with its vista of blue ocean and in the distance the striking cliffs of the peninsula, lush green interspersed with picturesque hamlets, which were tiny dots seen from this far away.

She was living a dream. She was here, with Alessandro, making love to him, having him turn her on in ways that were unimaginable. Why shouldn't she stuff reality behind a door and enjoy what was on offer for its brief duration?

She smiled, moved against his mouth and smiled more when he raised his head and chastised her for moving too fast.

'More doctor's orders?' she teased breathlessly.

'You said it.'

It felt to her as though she had been building up to this moment for years, from the very first time she had had that first latte with him, a sneaky, stolen latte. She had nervously told herself that it would be a one-off, that she was in no position to have lattes with him or with anyone else, but then, as now, what she had told herself had had no bearing on what had actually transpired.

They had had the most sexually charged yet chaste relationship on the planet. Every touch had been accidental and every touch had left her craving more. She had dreamt about him back then and had been terrified that Shaun would somehow climb into her head and see her dreams. And he had continued to steal into her dreams like a silent intruder all through the years, long after she had picked up the pieces of her life and moved on.

So now she was ready.

'Alessandro…' she breathed huskily and he lifted his head to look at her.

'Alessandro what…?' The spoils of the victor. Triumph surged through him. This was what he had wanted: to hear her plead for him to enter her, to know that she could no longer hold out. The grieving widow shedding her black and getting back into mainstream life. With him.

'Tell me how much you want me,' he encouraged thickly. 'I want to hear you say it. No, hold that thought—but don't even begin to think that you can start cooling down.' There were condoms in his wallet. He couldn't fetch one fast enough. His erection was so hard that it was painful.

Cool down? Chase thought that she wouldn't have cooled down if a barrel of ice cubes had been thrown over her. She was on fire, burning for him. She looked at him hungrily, watching as he put on the condom, enjoying the way he was looking right back at her, his dark eyes bold and wicked.

'I'd better just check…' he murmured, straddling her on the super-sized lounger which could have been made for sex and—who knew?—possibly had been because it was as comfortable as a bed. 'Make sure you're still hot for me…' He slid his finger expertly over her throbbing centre and gave a slashing smile of satisfaction. 'Hot and wet.'

'I'm glad you approve.' She wound her arms around his neck and pulled him down to her. Her nipples rubbing against him were doing all sorts of delicious things to her body, adding to the overload of sensation. She sighed and arched up so that she could kiss him and simultaneously opened her legs. 'God, Alessandro, I want you so much right now…'

'Are you sure?'

Their eyes met and she knew that he was asking her if she was ready. Given half a chance, he was always more than prepared to tell her the depth of his bitterness towards her, to inform her that her place in his life was temporary, a passing virus of which he needed to rid his system. Yet, as now, when she could see old-fashioned consideration in his eyes which could flare up almost against his will, he could be just so damned three-dimensional.

'I'm sure.'

Alessandro thrust into her and never had anything felt so exquisite. She wrapped her legs around his waist and he levered her up, his hand on her bottom, so that she could receive him even better as he began moving, fast and hard and rhythmically. Her fingers were digging into his back, driving him on, and her head was thrown back, her eyes closed, her mouth slightly parted.

For a split second, he had a crazy desire to know whether she had ever felt like this with her husband. He certainly had never felt like this with any other woman but, then again, what other woman had he ever had under such extraordinary circumstances? His last girlfriend, a model whose appearance in his life had not outlived the three-month mark, had been a clone of all the other beauties he had dated in the past. Was it any wonder that this one was special? That *this* just felt so damned special?

Chase had died and gone to heaven. On one final thrust, she tipped over the edge as her orgasm ripped through her, sending her body into little convulsions and spontaneously bringing tears to her eyes which she fought to blink back. She felt his groan of fulfilment with every ounce of her being and never had she wanted more to tell him how she felt. Instead, she swept his hair back and smiled drowsily as he opened his eyes to look at her, at first unfocused, and then smiling back.

'That was…good…' she murmured as he slid onto his side to prop himself up on one elbow so that he could look at her.

'"Good" is not an adjective I've ever had much time for. It's along the same lines as "nice"...' He idly circled her nipple with his finger and watched as it responded with enthusiasm. 'How *good* was it?'

'Very, very good…'

'I'll settle for that. In fact, I'll enjoy trying to squeeze more superlatives out of you.' He dipped his head and closed his mouth over her nipple, which was still sensitive and throbbing in the aftermath of their love-making. He was utterly spent and yet he felt himself stir against her leg. 'Let's have a swim,' he suggested. 'And then some food. And then we can play it by ear; see what comes up…'

'Oh, very funny.' But she was laughing as they jumped into the pool. After four lengths, she was happy to take to the side and watch as he continued to slice through the water. She had learned to swim as an adult. Four years ago, she wouldn't have been able to jump into the deep end of this pool, never mind swim four lengths. He, on the other hand, had probably been swimming since he was a toddler, taught by a member of staff in one of the many pools he had probably enjoyed in various locations over the years.

The differences between them were so glaringly obvious, reminding her of the shelf life of what they had and of the shadowy undercurrents lurking just beneath the surface of their sexually charged relationship.

'Tired?'

'Swimming isn't one of my strong points,' she confessed. 'In fact…' what would this one simple admission hurt? '…I only learned to swim a few years ago.'

'You're kidding.'

'No, I'm not,' she said with a shrug.

'That must have been awkward on family holidays. I'm surprised your parents didn't sort that out.' He kissed her again, a little more hungrily this time, and pulled back with a grin of pure satisfaction. 'Besides, don't schools in England have arranged swimming lessons for kids? Something to do with the curriculum?'

'Some of them do,' Chase said vaguely. 'But, you know, I kind of had a phobia of water.'

'A little private tuition would have sorted that out, wouldn't it?' He swung himself neatly out of the pool and held out his hand to help her up. 'Better than Mummy and Daddy panicking every time their precious little darling got within a foot of the hotel pool. Hmm…nice…'

He enjoyed her wet body, running his hands along it, holding her close to him so that their bodies could rub together. 'No matter. Competitive swimming isn't on the agenda while we're here. I couldn't care less if you can only swim four lengths or four hundred.'

Chase opened her mouth, toyed with the idea of revealing a bit more about herself but then kept silent. This fantastic side to Alessandro was only in evidence for a reason.

Further proof of her lying would kill that reason dead because, even for the sake of finishing unfinished business, lust still had its outer limits. And without lust how much greater would be his anger in the cold light of day? She didn't want his anger and she certainly couldn't afford for that anger to be directed at punishing her through her work.

A sudden tidal wave of sheer misery immobilised her and it took almost more effort than she could muster to get herself back on track.

'Tell me what there is around here,' she eventually said, falling easily into step with him as he tossed her a towel and they began walking towards the house. 'All those gorgeous little villages… What do the locals do for a living? Do you know any of them? Personally, I mean?'

Exactly four days later, Chase understood what it must feel like to be in love with someone, living on cloud nine, where everything smelled differently and tasted differently and every single experience was a unique Kodak moment to be committed to memory and brought out at a later date.

She had seen him at his most relaxed. She felt that she could almost be forgiven for thinking that he really liked her and she guessed that, in a way, he did. He appreciated her quick mind; he appreciated her responsive body; he laughed when she tried to tell corny jokes.

Just so long as they both pretended that the past had never happened, everything was good between them. For her, it was so much deeper than anything he could possibly feel, but she refused to think like that. What was the point? She had made her bed and she would lie on it. She had accepted his proposal and only now and again did she think that, whilst she was falling deeper and harder for him, he was gradually working her out of his system.

Wrapped up in his arms at night, lying in a bed that was roughly the size of her spare bedroom, she had let her mind wander, analysed and re-analysed everything he'd said and every gesture he'd made. The one sure thing that sprang to mind was that, the more relaxed he was with her, the more he was putting her behind him.

It was an argument that made sense. When he had seen her again for the first time after eight years, his rage had been raw, out in the open, targeted and deadly. But that had changed. He would never, ever forgive her for what she had done to him, she knew that, but he was in the process of getting over it. Rage was becoming indifference and indifference was allowing him to stop treating her as public enemy number one.

She hated herself for trying to find alternative scenarios but they all led to the same dead end. Very soon, he would completely lose interest in why she had done what she had done eight years ago. He would simply stop giving a damn. He would no longer consider revenge because he would not care less. He would just use her and walk away without a backward glance.

The only consolation was that she had not dropped her guard. She had not let him see just how vulnerable she was, nor would she let him discover how successful he had been at claiming the revenge he had initially considered his due. Without him even realising it, he had indeed wreaked the ultimate revenge, because he would leave her broken and in pieces, whatever show of bravado she employed for his benefit.

And now here they were, last night, sitting across from each other at the kitchen table with an almost empty bottle of Chablis between them.

'So tell me again why you don't come here at least once a month, Alessandro.' Outside, another hot day had gradually morphed into a mild, starry night. They had spent most nights in the kitchen, which was huge, big enough for a ten-seater table at one end, and leading to a conservatory which doubled as an informal sitting area with comfy sofas and a plasma television. From here, they had an uninterrupted view of the sea down below, vast and silent, and the small back garden where they had spent much of their time by the swimming pool.

She felt lazy and replete after another excellent meal which had been prepared in advance by his housekeeper. They could have done their own cooking, and she had suggested it on day one, but he had killed that dead.

'Why waste time cooking?' he had questioned bluntly, 'When there are so many other things we could be occupied doing?' He had pulled her onto his lap and slipped his finger underneath her panties, leaving her in no doubt as to what those other things they could be occupied with were. Enjoying any form of domesticity was off the cards. That was not the reason why he had asked her on this holiday.

'You know why I don't come here once a month,' he replied wryly. 'It's the same reason *you* wouldn't come here once a month. Work wouldn't allow it.'

'But it's different for you. You're the big boss. You can do whatever you want. I can't.'

'Pull the other one, Chase. You're not a bimbo who would be content to while away her time walking barefoot on a beach, no matter how powdery white the sand might be. You're one hundred per cent a career woman. You would be bored stiff in a job that allowed you to take time out every month to enjoy a holiday in the sunshine.'

He stood up, moved to the fridge to replenish the wine and remained there with his back against the counter, carefully looking at her with his head to one side. She had caught the sun. Her skin was the colour of pale honey and from nowhere a smattering of freckles had appeared on the ridge of her nose.

'I recognised that the first time I laid eyes on you,' he continued casually. 'You weren't going to be distracted by anyone or anything. You barely seemed to notice what was going on around you.'

Chase fidgeted. Trips down memory lane never turned out well between them. However, his voice was mild and speculative, not in the least provocative. More proof that, whatever fireworks there might be on the physical level, on the emotional level he was breaking away. The medicine was working. Sex was finishing the unfinished business between them.

'I liked that,' he continued and she looked at him in surprise. 'You once asked me if I'd ever go out with a career woman and I gave you a negative answer.' He strolled towards her and resumed his seat at the kitchen table, tugging a free chair with his foot so that he could use it as an impromptu footrest. 'The truth is, you were the anomaly. Before you and after you, I've only gone out with…'

'Airheads? Bimbos?' Chase dropped into the brief silence. She smiled tightly. 'Women who are never ashamed to admit that their only ambition is to hunt down a rich guy and bag him even if it means a lifetime of doing exactly what he wants her to do?' The stuff of nightmares, she thought bitterly.

'There's absolutely nothing about a woman like that I can't handle, and you'd be surprised how easily they've slotted into my lifestyle.'

'Because they make sure to always tell you what you want to hear and do what you want them to do?'

'Some might say that a compliant woman is preferable to a liar.' He noted the swift surge of colour that flooded her cheeks. 'You *have* succeeded in persuading me, however, that there's something to be said for a woman with a brain.'

'I have?'

'You have,' Alessandro drawled. 'Don't get me wrong, Chase—agile though your mind is, and challenging though your conversation can be, you'll never be a contender for the vacancy—just in case your thoughts were heading in that direction.'

'They weren't!' Chase was mortified to think that he might have spotted some weakness in her armour that she hadn't been able to conceal. 'You're not dealing with an idiot, Alessandro. I know the rules of this game as well as you do.'

'I'm glad to hear it.'

'Why would you have thought any differently?' Just like that, his dark eyes had turned cool and assessing, reminding her that the so-called rules of this particular game were different for both of them, despite what she might say to the contrary. Reminding her, too, that his red-hot passion had changed nothing of what he fundamentally felt towards her.

'Look around you and tell me what you see.'

'We're in your kitchen.' Chase frowned, confused and flustered by the softly spoken question that seemed to have sprung from nowhere. 'I can just about make out the little garden at the back, and I can see where the pool is… Look, why are you asking me this?'

'What you see all around you is evidence of my wealth,' Alessandro inserted smoothly. He killed dead the passing twinge of hesitation at the thought that he might offend her. He reminded himself that no matter how good the sex was, and how much he might occasionally enjoy her rapier-sharp mind, she was still a woman whom he had met going by the name of Lyla; who had strung him along and lied to him; who had dumped him unceremoniously and who, certainly, he would never have clapped eyes on again had fate not decided to deliver her to his premises. At the end of the day, whether he offended her or not was immaterial.

'But,' he continued as she stared at him, perplexed, 'I

guess you were aware of the extent of my bank balance the minute you walked into my London place.'

'I don't see what your bank balance has to do with anything,' Chase said tautly.

'No? Let's just say that I wouldn't want you to start getting any misplaced ideas.'

'Misplaced ideas about what?' But she knew what he was talking about now. Well, it didn't take a genius to join the dots, did it? She should be enraged, but instead she was deeply hurt, cut to the quick.

'This is all about the sex—and it's great sex, I'll give you that. But don't think for a second that I've somehow forgotten the person you really are. I think this is a good point at which to remind you that you're a visitor in my life. You won't be getting your hands on any of this…' He gestured broadly to encompass the visible proof of his vast wealth.

He couldn't have thought of a more pointed way of humiliating her but she pinned a stiff smile to her face. She hoped she looked suitably amused and unimpressed. She hoped that whatever expression she was wearing revealed nothing of what she was actually feeling.

'Do you think I would actually *want* to be anything other than a…what did you call it, Alessandro?… *visitor* in your life?' Her heart contracted, squeezed tight with pain. 'You might have all…' she mimicked his gesture '…*this.* You might have the fabulous house on a fabulous coastline in a fabulously beautiful country, and you might have a house in London big enough to fit ten of mine, but I've never pursued money and I certainly would never, ever, set my sights on getting hold of someone else's by…'

'Fair means or foul?' He took his time standing up, flexing his muscles while watching her. Then he leant across to place his hands flat on the arms of her chair. 'I felt it a good idea to make sure we were both still singing off the same song sheet.'

'I could never be serious about someone as arrogant as you, Alessandro.'

'And yet you gave such a misleading impression eight years ago.'

'Will you ever forget that?'

'It's been imprinted on my mind with the force and clarity of a branding iron.'

So much for thinking that he was becoming indifferent, Chase was forced to concede. So much for thinking that revenge was a dish in which he might no longer be interested. 'You weren't arrogant then.' She met his stare levelly. She wasn't prepared for the feel of his mouth against hers as he crushed her lips in a driving, savage kiss that propelled her back into the chair.

Her hands automatically rose to push him away. How the hell could he think that she might be interested in having him touch her when he had just insulted her in the worst way possible? And yet her body responded, went up in flames like dry tinder waiting for the burning match. Reluctant hands softened to cup the nape of his neck.

In one easy movement, he scooped her off the chair and into his arms.

'Alessandro!'

He was heading up the stairs, towards the bedroom with its shuttered windows and thin, cream voile curtains, pale wood and wicker furniture.

'We've talked enough.'

'You called me a gold-digger! Do you…?' She was breathless as he kicked open the bedroom door. 'Do you honestly think that I…I get turned on being insulted?'

'I didn't call you a gold-digger. I warned you of the pitfalls of becoming one. And, no, you don't get turned on by being insulted. You just get turned on by me…' He unceremoniously dumped her on the bed and shot her a wickedly sexy smile as she scrambled into a sitting position to glare at him. 'I'm sick of talking.' He stripped off his black polo shirt and flung it to the floor. 'Get naked for me.'

Chase continued to glare but already her flustered mind was forgetting the hurt inflicted and keening towards the feel of his hands on her body. Still, she didn't rush to obey, but as he led the way, removing his shirt then his jeans, she could feel herself melting.

Their love-making was fast and urgent. She wanted to lose herself in it and forget the things he had told her, the coldness in his voice when he had reminded her of what their relationship really was all about. Did he honestly imagine that she was the type of woman who could look at someone else's possessions and work out how she could get her hands on them? Yes, of course he did. The distance between a liar and a gold-digger was very small.

She wanted to make love until she lost the hurt, and she did. She touched him, kissed him, dominating him in one move before yielding in another. She caught a glimpse of his back at one point and saw the marks of where her fingers had scored into his skin. He ordered her to talk dirty to him and she wondered how she did it so easily when she hadn't a clue what she was supposed to say. It was a complete release of all her inhibitions and it turned her on. It turned her on even more when he talked dirty back to her.

This was what it was all about—having sex. The most amazing, fulfilling sex she could ever imagine. It was all he wanted and, if it wasn't all *she* wanted, then that was something she would just have to live with.

Her orgasm was long and deep and filled every single part of her body. It dispelled all her dark thoughts. It made her feel as though she was soaring through space, out of reach of anything that might hurt her. She longed for it to last for ever. In fact, she closed her eyes and kept them firmly shut even after Alessandro rolled off her. He was breathing as unevenly as she was. She could picture every inch of his face, every line, the sweep of his dark lashes, his gleaming black eyes that could make her body go up in flames with a single glance. She had absorbed all the details and stored them in her head with the efficiency of a state-of-the-art computer housing data.

'Are you going to fall asleep on me?'

'I'm dozing.'

'Should I be flattered that I can send a woman to sleep?'

'Actually…' Chase opened her eyes reluctantly and propped herself on her side so that they were facing one another on the bed, front to front, her breasts brushing his chest. 'I was thinking…'

What would happen if she ever told him the truth about how she felt? Would she find it liberating? 'About work. How much I'll have to get done when I return. I may even go in tomorrow evening after we're back. Have I told you about the work that's due to start on the shelter? Beth keeps asking if I'm sure that the costs will be covered.' She ran her finger lightly along his shoulder blade, tracing muscle and sinew. 'She has a morbid fear of bailiffs banging on the front door because she hasn't been able to pay her creditors.'

Alessandro frowned. As pillow talk went, it left a lot to be desired, yet he realised that he should be feeling relieved. He had laid down his dictates and she hadn't blinked an eye. In fact, he need not have bothered. She had no interest in taking things between them beyond their natural course. Thank God. And, to prove how misguided he had been in imagining that she might get a little too wrapped up in *this,* here she was now, chatting about work. Did it get less romantic?

But who the hell wanted romance? 'I need a shower,' he said abruptly.

'Are you okay? I shouldn't have mentioned the shelter. I wouldn't want you to think that I don't trust you…' She sat up, slightly panicked by his sudden mood swing, and it occurred to her that this was something she would have to get accustomed to if she decided to stick it out. He didn't care about her. Why should it bother him if he was dismissive, if he decided to have a mood swing?

'You clearly have a way to go if you think that I would ever back down on my word, despite my assurances.' Alessandro eased himself off the bed. 'I can bring the flight forward if you have work issues. In fact, might not be a bad idea. I have a couple of major deals about to reach boiling point. I need to be back sooner rather than later. A few hours makes all the difference sometimes.'

Suddenly backed into a corner, Chase nodded brightly. 'I'll begin packing while you're in the shower.' She waited for him to relent, to tell her that they should stick to the original timetable; what did a few hours matter? He didn't.

And what happened with them when they returned? It was a question she was reluctant to ask.

It hovered at the back of her mind for the remainder of the night and through into the following morning. Flights had been rescheduled and still nothing was said and she refused to weaken. His mood had disappeared as fast as it had come. On the surface, everything was bright and breezy. When she looked back at the villa from the back of the limo as they were driving away, she felt a pang of intense sadness that she would never see it again.

He seemed to be lost in his own thoughts and she acknowledged that he was probably projecting ahead, thinking about those deals of his that wouldn't go away unless he was on the scene to sort them out.

The silence between them became oppressive but it was

only when they had touched down at Heathrow that she turned to him and said lightly, 'So, what happens next…?'

Alessandro had had no idea how tense he had been until she asked that question. He had been infuriated with himself for not much liking her air of casual insouciance. Did the woman give a damn one way or another? But now, his keen ears tuning in to a thread of nervousness in her voice, he was satisfied that she did, and that did wonders for his ego.

'I'll call you.' He curved a sure hand on her cheek and bent to place a hungry kiss on her lips.

Chase was ashamed of the enthusiasm with which she returned his kiss. If she could have, she would have dragged him off to the nearest hotel room and picked up where they had left off in Italy. Instead, she pulled away with a sigh. 'I've never had much time for those women who hang around waiting for the phone to ring.'

Alessandro laughed. Her kiss conveyed a thousand messages and all of them were good. 'I haven't had enough of you by a long shot. I'll call you tomorrow. Save you doing too much waiting by the phone…although, if you *do* find yourself waiting by the phone, then give my imagination something to go on. It would work if you waited there in your birthday suit…'

So what if she hadn't said anything? Would he have posed the question himself? Would he have wanted to know what happened next? Was this going to be her destiny for the foreseeable future—a day-to-day existence, only coming alive when Alessandro was around; not daring to breathe a word of how she really felt; living in fear of the phone calls stopping, grateful for whatever crumbs continued to drop her way? Was this what she had spent the past eight years working towards?

She took a taxi back to the house. She couldn't face the vagaries of the underground.

It was a little after two in the afternoon by the time she was paying the taxi driver. A thin, annoying drizzle had started, accompanied by a gusty wind, and as she fumbled in her handbag for her keys there was nothing on her mind other than getting inside the house and out of the rain.

She certainly wasn't expecting the man that stepped out of the shadows at the side of the house. When he spoke, all thoughts of the rain, getting inside and even of Alessandro flew out of her head. She gaped in horror as he smiled and pulled his hoodie down a little lower so that most of his face was in shadow.

'Long time no see, Chase. Been anywhere exciting…?'

CHAPTER EIGHT

CHASE WOKE WITH a start to the sound of her alarm going off. She had a few seconds of intense disorientation and then memories of the afternoon before broke through the barrier of forgetfulness and began pouring through her head. She had no idea how she had managed to get through what remained of the day, how she had managed finally to get to sleep.

She began getting ready for work on autopilot, showering, fetching her smart grey suit from the wardrobe, twinning it with a crisp white shirt. When half an hour later she looked at her reflection in the mirror, on the surface she was the same diligent, nicely dressed professional her colleagues would be expecting back at the office after a few days in the sun, with a companion or companions unknown.

Under the surface, she was barely functioning.

She had not expected to return to her house and find Brian Shepherd on her doorstep. In fact, she had not expected ever to have set eyes on Brian Shepherd again, but then didn't bad things have a habit of bouncing right back? Wasn't it true what they said, that you could run but you couldn't hide?

She had foolishly imagined Brian Shepherd to be nothing but a distant memory from the bad old days. 'Blue Boy' had been his nickname, because of his bright-blue eyes. He had been Shaun's closest friend growing up, the one who, from the age of ten, had shown him all the clever ways they could break and enter houses and all the tricks of the trade for getting their hands on valuable scrap metal. Six years older than Shaun, he had been his mentor until finally she and Shaun had moved to London, leaving behind Blue Boy for good. Fat chance, as it turned out.

And now he was back.

'Heard you were doing well for yourself,' he had said, inviting himself into her house and scanning it with the shrewd eyes of a born petty thief. 'Heard you found yourself a replacement for Shaunie.'

She had flinched every time he had reached out to touch one of her possessions but past experience had taught her that any sign of weakness would be a mistake with Brian Shepherd. She knew all about his temper.

There had been no need to ask him how he had found out about Alessandro. He had volunteered the information with relish: a friend of a friend of a friend had spotted them together on their little love-bird holiday in Italy. At the airport, of all places. Wasn't it a small world?

'Angie—Angie Carson. Remember her? Fat cow. Took a picture of the both of you. On her phone. Bet you never spotted her! Probably wouldn't have recognised her cos it's been a while, hasn't it? Anyone would think you were ashamed of all your old mates…'

He didn't remove his hoodie the entire time he was at the house, prowling through from room to room, touching and picking things up and turning them round in his hands, as though trying to figure out what they were worth.

Chase remained largely silent until, eventually, when she could stand it no longer, she asked him what he wanted, because of course he would want something.

Money. He was in a bit of a tight spot. Just enough to tide him over, and he knew she could lay her hands on some, because they'd driven off in a flash car and the luggage…

He gave a low, long whistle and eyed her up and down in a way that made her stomach lurch. Nice luggage. Expensive. Angie had been impressed. Snapped a few pics of that on her phone and all.

So, just a bit of money, spare change for a bloke who could zoom off in a chauffeur-driven limo with all that nice luggage in the boot. Angie had gone off with her mates but he was betting that, wherever that flash car had driven to, it wasn't going to be a one-star dump with dodgy air-conditioning.

So, what did she say? Did she think that she could spare an old friend a bit of loose change? Maybe, he said, he could persuade her. He knew where she worked…had done a little digging after those photos fat Angie had shown him…

Remember that club, the one that got busted by the coppers….? Course, she'd been underage at the time and she hadn't actually been doing drugs or anything—not like him and Shaunie and the rest of the gang. But those posh people at the law firm, they'd be really keen to know that she used to mix with a crowd who all had police records, wouldn't they? Might even get to thinking that *she* had a police record! Wouldn't that be funny? And, being honest, just the fact that she and he used to be mates would get them wondering, wouldn't it?

He had chuckled. 'You know what they say about the smelly stuff sticking…'

Her mobile rang now just as she was about to enter the office. Alessandro. She switched it off. There was no way that she could talk to him. Not just yet. But talk to him she would have to, because Brian Shepherd wasn't going to go away until he got his wretched money which, as it turned out, was hardly what she would have called 'loose change'.

It was certainly more than she had set aside, which was precious little after her mortgage repayments had been made and the bills paid.

Her life seemed to be unravelling at speed and she had to force herself not to succumb to the meltdown she knew was hovering just around the corner. She had weathered a lot of things and she would weather this as well. It would just take a little working out.

By the time she pushed through the doors to their offices, she had glumly decided what needed to be done.

Her first port of call was her boss's office.

Tony Grey was a short, round man in his fifties who would have been a dead ringer for Father Christmas were it not for the fact that he was almost entirely bald and his dark-grey eyes were way too astute for someone who spent all his time laughing and chuckling. In actual fact, Chase had never seen her boss laugh out loud, but he had always been fair and supportive. She would miss that.

She would have to hand in her notice. She had come to that conclusion as she had left her house. Brian Shepherd wouldn't just do what he threatened; he would go further if she didn't do as he asked. Hadn't he been banged up for nearly killing someone in a bar brawl when he was fourteen? What if he took it into his head to release his explosive temper on *her* if she didn't play ball? If he could nearly kill someone at the age of fourteen because they'd accidentally knocked into him without saying sorry, then he could certainly kill her if he wanted money from her and she refused to pay. She loathed the thought of having to yield in a situation like this but pride was no match for sheer common sense.

Well, on the bright side, she would find a company specialising more in the pro bono work she enjoyed and, even if Brian hunted her down there, he would be able to see for himself that it wasn't a money-making machine.

She still couldn't work out how he had discovered her whereabouts but there was no point wasting time trying to figure that out. With social-networking sites stretching their tentacles into every area of everyone's lives, it wouldn't have been beyond the wit of man for him to ferret her out the second he'd figured he could get money from her.

'My dear,' Tony said when she had explained that she would have to hand in her notice for personal reasons. 'Are you sure this is really what you want to do? You're on course to go far with this firm. Your dedication is second to none.'

But he assured her that, if he couldn't persuade her to change her mind, then of course he would provide her with glowing references. With just that sympathy and fairness which she would miss so much, he also agreed that she could leave as soon as she had tied up loose ends on the cases she was currently working on so that they could be handed over in good order.

She had no idea what he concluded her 'personal reasons' for leaving might be, but she suspected that health issues might be at the heart of it, and he was right in a way. She certainly wasn't feeling very well at the moment. Not when she considered the way her nicely controlled life had been turned upside down.

Alessandro… She thought that this might not be as similarly smooth sailing. She ignored a further two calls from him, only picking up his last just as she was about to leave the office on the dot of five. Clock watching had never been her style, but tying up loose ends was a dismal procedure. Nor was she up to chatting to all and sundry about her decision to leave.

'Where the hell have you been? I've phoned three times!'

'I'm sorry. I was…busy.' Just the sound of his voice

sent little ripples of awareness racing up and down her spine as she took the lift to the ground floor and emerged into yet another cool and overcast day to do battle with public transport.

'Busy doing what?'

'I, well, I've handed in my notice at Fitzsimmons.'

For a few seconds, Alessandro debated whether he had heard her correctly. But there was something in her voice, a tell-tale tremor that she couldn't quite conceal; a nuance which he felt that only he would have been able to pick up. Something was different, *wrong,* a little off-kilter.

He stood up, restlessly moving away from his desk towards the windows and absently looking down. 'You're kidding.'

'No, I'm not. Can we meet? I can…um…come to your office.'

'I can think of a better venue.'

'I'd rather your office, Alessandro.'

'What's going on?' he demanded bluntly. 'And please don't tell me *nothing.* You tell me you've handed in your notice, even though you've expressed nothing but satisfaction at your job there, and now…you want to meet me *in my office*?'

'Please.'

Alessandro sighed heavily and raked his fingers through his hair. He was getting a very bad vibe about whatever the hell was going on but he acquiesced. Whatever was happening, he would be able to get it out of her and things would return to normal. He was nothing if not wholly confident in his ability to take her mind off things.

'I'd rather not parade my personal life in front of my employees,' he drawled. 'And *you* may be scuttling out of the office because you've handed in your notice and lost momentum in your job, but my people are all still at their desks. If you can't wait until later and meet me somewhere private, then I can see you in forty-five minutes at that brasserie round the corner from my office. You know the one?'

She did. She made her way there slowly, forgoing the speed and ease of a black cab in favour of a laborious trip by public transport. It suited her mood.

How had life changed so fast in such a brief moment in time? As she neared the brasserie, she felt a sickening lurch of déjà vu. Eight years ago she had met Alessandro here with one thing and one thing only in her head—the need to get rid of him. She had walked towards a conversation she had known would break her in half and she was doing the same thing now. History was repeating itself. But it was so much worse this time, she would be taking so many more regrets with her when she was finished saying what she had to say.

Sitting at the back of the brasserie, nursing an extremely early glass of red wine, Alessandro had been waiting for ten minutes. He had been unable to get down to work after her phone call. He would never have imagined himself as one of those sensitive, intuitive sorts but something wasn't right and, however much he told himself that he could sort out whatever the hell it was that was eating her up, he was still vaguely uneasy.

And yet, why should he be? They had parted company the day before and everything had been just fine and dandy. There'd been no inconvenient intuition then. So, really, what could have materially changed since then?

He spotted her the second she walked through the door. For the briefest of moments he felt a sharp, inexplicable pang of nostalgia for the carefree girl in shorts and tee-shirts who had been his companion for the past few days. She was in full lawyer mode: prissy grey suit, even prissier white blouse, black pumps. He wondered how long he could wait before he ripped the whole lot off her and bedded her.

On cue, his erection pushed hard against the zip of his trousers and he shifted position uncomfortably to release some of the insistent ache in his groin.

He had not expected this crazy lust to be an ongoing situation after the countless times they had now slept together. He had assumed she would be more than just disposable: he would take what had once been denied him and then discard her without preamble. It wasn't working out quite as he had envisaged, but he shrugged that off. The unexpected could sometimes be a good thing and getting turned on by her on a semi-permanent basis was definitely not to be sneezed at, especially for him, a man whose tastes had become lamentably jaded over time.

He watched with masculine appreciation as she glanced around her. Already he was undressing her in his mind. Slowly. Revealing those generous pale breasts inch by succulent inch; exposing the pink nipples to take them one at a time in his mouth as they pouted temptingly up at him.

He pictured the prissy grey skirt hitting the ground, followed by whatever suitably functional underwear she happened to be wearing… He could almost taste the honeyed sweetness between her legs, hear her broken little whimpers of pleasure as his tongue found her sweet spot and worked it until the broken little whimpers became moans and cries of pleasure. The more horny he became, just sitting and watching her and letting his imagination run wild, the faster he knew he would have to sort out whatever was on her mind just so that he could get her back to his place. They might not even be able to make it to the bedroom.

He grinned as she spotted him and lazily attracted the waitress's attention without taking his eyes off Chase's face. Her looks were really quite startling. There was a sexiness to her, a perfection to her features, that made her naturally guarded expression all the more beguiling. He could see other men surreptitiously following her with their eyes as she weaved her way towards him.

'Alessandro…' Chase said weakly. She could feel her heart thumping like a sledgehammer inside her.

'So you've handed in your notice.' He broke off to order her a cappuccino. 'And you don't look very happy about it.'

'I…I…' She could barely string two words together. This was so much worse than she had envisaged. There was just no way that she could pretend to be cool, calm and collected. Her nerves were all over the place.

'Sit down. Tell me about it. Why?'

'I…I didn't have much of a choice,' she admitted truthfully. 'Personal reasons.'

'What personal reasons?'

'I'd rather not talk about it.'

'Are you ill?' He felt a sudden mixture of fear and irrational panic. 'Is that what this is all about?'

'No,' she said, waving a wistful goodbye to what could have been a fantastic excuse. As if lies hadn't landed her here in the first place. 'No, I'm not ill.'

'Then what? What personal reasons, and why don't you want to discuss them?' Alessandro scowled. Since when had he ever been interested in women's life stories? Mysteries dangling at the end of a line like bait to hook him in had always left him cold.

He eyed her narrowly as a new thought began to take shape in his head. 'If you're not ill,' he said slowly, 'and yet you've reluctantly had to hand in your notice, then there's only one explanation that springs to mind…'

Temporarily diverted, Chase looked at him in bafflement. 'Is there?'

'Someone's made a pass at you. Who is it?' His voice was low and controlled but he clenched his fists. The second he had a name, he would personally make it his business to make sure that the culprit paid.

'Made a pass at me?'

'Even wearing that starchy suit, you're still sexy as hell, Chase. And I won't be the only one who can see that. So, spill the beans. Tell me who it is. Your boss? One of your colleagues? What did he do? Did he touch you inappropriately? Try to feel you up?'

He imagined one of those rich kids thinking that he could have a go at the sexiest woman in the office and he was overwhelmed by an explosive rage. He had met enough twenty-something lawyers in his time to know that the majority of them thought that they were studs.

'No one touched me, Alessandro! And no one tried to *feel me up*! Do you think that I'm so feeble that I would allow anyone to get away with that? Do you think that I'm incapable of taking care of myself?' But his show of possessiveness touched her. She folded her hands on her lap to stop herself from reaching out and covering his hand with her own.

'Then what's going on?' Looking at her, it was clear that she could barely meet his eyes. She was fidgeting nervously with the handle of her coffee cup. Alessandro felt that he could do with the entire bottle of wine, never mind one careful glass. Instead he ordered a black coffee while he tried to sift through some plausible explanation for her behaviour in his mind. 'You're not…pregnant, are you?' It was a thought that only now occurred to him.

Chase glanced up at his face, suddenly ashen, and for a few moments anger replaced gnawing anxiety and dread. It was obvious from his expression that the mere suggestion of pregnancy had knocked him for six. 'And what if I *was*?' she queried boldly. 'What if I told you that there was a mini-Alessandro taking shape right now inside me?'

She fancied she could see the colour drain away from

his face as she allowed him time to absorb the full horror of that scenario. 'Don't worry, Alessandro. I'm not pregnant. I told you once that I'm not a complete idiot.'

For a few fleeting seconds, Alessandro had found himself ripped out of his comfort zone, staring down the barrel of a gun. She was having his baby. *His baby.* The gun barrel, strangely, was less of a threat than he might have imagined.

'Accidents happen,' he said grimly.

'Oh, Alessandro…' She sighed and sat back, head tilted up, eyes half-closed as the inescapable hurtled towards her with the deadly force of a bomb. 'I'm healthy, there's no mini-Alessandro on the way and no one's made a pass at me at work. And I wish there was some other way of saying this but there isn't…' She straightened and took a deep breath. 'I need to ask you something.'

'What?'

'I need to…borrow some money from you.'

Deathly silence greeted this request. Chase didn't dare look at Alessandro. What choice did she have? she wondered helplessly. Brian wasn't going to go away until he had his money and she simply didn't have it. If she got it, gave it to him and then convinced him that she had broken up with Alessandro, then he would go away. If she didn't, then she was, frankly, scared of what he might do. Scared of all the old horrors landing on her doorstep once again.

'Tell me I'm not hearing this.'

'I'm sorry and, naturally, I'll pay you back every penny of what I borrow. With interest.'

Alessandro laughed mirthlessly. 'So finally,' he said in a lethally soft voice, 'the real face of Chase Evans is revealed. I'm surprised you managed to keep it hidden for so long.' He felt as though he had been punched in the gut. This wasn't just anger; this was a level of hurt that he could barely acknowledge even to himself. He didn't know who he loathed more—himself for having been conned a second time, or her for having been the one to do the conning.

'What do you need the money for?' He could scarcely credit that he was willing to hear her out, willing to give her an explanation that would allow him to make sense of the situation. That window of willingness died the second she looked at him and said steadily,

'I'm sorry. That's…none of your business.' The harshest of words, yet they would provide the clean break.

'Right. So…when did you decide that you could screw me for money?' he asked in the same ultra-controlled voice that was far more intimidating than if he had stood up and shouted at her. 'Was it when you came to my house? Or was it when we went to Italy and you saw just how much I had? Tell me. I'm curious.'

'You don't understand, Alessandro. I wouldn't be sitting here asking you for money if…if…I didn't have to.'

'And yet you refuse to tell me what you want the money for.' He threw up his hands in rampant frustration as she greeted this with stubborn silence. 'Are you in some sort of debt? Hell, Chase, just be bloody straight with me!'

'I told you, it's none of your business. If you don't want to lend me the money, then just say so.' Her heart was breaking in two.

'And, just for the record, how much money do you fancy you can bleed me for?'

She named the figure and watched as he threw his head back and roared with laughter, except there was no humour there. He was laughing with incredulity and his dark eyes were as hard and cold as the frozen depths of a glacier.

'Well…?' Chase cleared her throat and valiantly met his eyes.

'No explanations, no excuses, not even of the make-believe variety… Sorry, not good enough.' He signalled to the waitress for the bill. 'And consider this conversation over.' Hell, the woman could act. She was as white as a sheet and her hands were shaking—remarkable performance. He felt something painful twist inside him, an iron fist clenching on his intestines, and staunched it down.

'I think we can say that our unfinished business has been concluded. If you ever get it into your head to descend on me, either at my offices or at my house, I assure you I will have you forcibly removed either by the police or by my security personnel. Do you read me?'

Chase nodded. Had she expected him to part with cash just because she'd asked? Because she'd offered to pay him back? Was there some part of her that had hoped he might know her well enough by now to give her the benefit of the doubt? She couldn't tell him the truth. How could she? She was boxed in with no room to manoeuvre.

'I understand,' she said quietly.

'Question.' Alessandro was furious with himself for not walking away without a backward glance. He was even more furious with himself for the unwilling tug of compassion he was feeling for a woman who was nothing more or less than a gold-digger with great acting ability. And, underneath that maelstrom of emotion, he recognised the angry pain of disillusionment. 'If you're so desperate for money, why jack the job in?'

'I can't discuss that either.'

Alessandro stood up abruptly. 'Good luck finding your money,' he told her coldly. 'If anything needs to be discussed about the shelter, you might want another lawyer to handle it.'

'I've already begun tidying up all my ongoing case files. Someone else will be handling all the details with the shelter. I…I've been given permission to leave at the end of the week. I should be working out a month's notice but my boss—'

'Not really interested.'

Chase remained standing, watching his departing back. She told herself, bracingly, that it was always going to end—yet the hollowness filling her felt as destructive as a tsunami. If she wasn't a homeowner, if she had been one of the millions renting, she knew that she would have upped sticks and disappeared. No job, no Alessandro and a threat waiting for her when she returned: it took all her courage to gather herself and head back outside down to the underground.

Brian would be there. He had told her in a chummy voice laced with menace that he would be waiting when she returned, that he didn't mind just hanging out there, although if she wanted to hand her key over to him…

Chase shuddered.

Heading in the opposite direction back to his office, Alessandro angrily realised that the very last thing he was in the mood to do was work. He still had a conference call lined up for later that evening. He got on his mobile, spoke to his secretary and cancelled it.

Hell, could he have been *that* stupid that he had fallen for the walk up the garden path *yet again*? With tremendous effort, he side-lined the fury raging through him and tried to recall the details of their brief conversation in the brasserie.

She hadn't given him an answer when he had asked her why she had handed in her notice if she needed money. That, for one thing, made no sense. Whatever debts she had managed to incur, she wasn't so stupid that she could imagine settling them without a regular salary coming in. So had she been sacked? Had they discovered something? Had she been embezzling? It seemed a ludicrous idea, but hell, how was he to know when she had offered no explanation for her behaviour?

No, this was not going to happen again. He was emphatically *not* going to be left stranded with a bucket load of unanswered questions, as had happened last time round. Whether he ever laid eyes on her again or not was immaterial. He would pay her a little visit and would stay put until she answered all his questions to his satisfaction. Then, and only then, would he leave.

He called his driver to collect him. Rush-hour traffic meant that it took a ridiculously long time before his driver made it to the building, even though his car, parked outside his house, was only a matter of a couple miles away as the crow flew. It took even longer to navigate the stand-still traffic in central London.

His mobile buzzed continuously and he eventually switched it off. He was fully given over to trying to disentangle the conversation he had had with Chase. He felt like a man in possession of just sufficient pieces of a complex puzzle to rouse curiosity and yet lacking the essential ones that would solve the conundrum.

This, he told himself, was why he was sitting in the back of his car, drumming his fingers restlessly on the leather seat and frowning out of the back window. He had been presented with a complex puzzle and it was only human nature to try and figure it out, whatever the cost. Frankly, he would drag answers out of her if he had to.

It was considerably later than he had expected by the time the car swung into her small road. From outside, he could see that lights were on. 'You can leave,' he told his driver. 'I'll get a cab back to my house.' He slammed the door and watched as the Jag slowly disappeared around the corner.

If there was a small voice in his head telling him that his appearance on her doorstep made little sense, given the fact that she had never been destined to be a permanent feature in his life, he chose to ignore it. Finding answers seemed more important than debating the finer points.

He leaned his hand on the doorbell and kept it there for an inordinately long time. Where the hell was she? If the lights were on, then she was home. She had a thing about wasting electricity, just one of her many little quirks to which he had become accustomed. He scowled at the very fact that he was remembering that at this juncture.

Chase heard the insistent buzzing of the doorbell but it took her a second or two before she generated the enthusiasm to get the door. In the lounge, a fuming Brian was filling a bin bag with whatever he fancied he could take from her. There was nothing she could do about it; he was bigger and he had no conscience when it came to violence.

She'd have done anything to get rid of him, to have him out of her house. He told her to get rid of whoever was at the door.

'Too busy here for visitors, darling. Still a lot to get through before I leave!'

Chase pulled open the door and her mouth fell open in shock. Alessandro was the last person she had expected to find on her doorstep.

'You're not getting rid of me until you tell me what the hell is really going on with you!' were his opening words.

'Alessandro, you have to go.'

She was scared stiff; that much he could see. He pushed past her and halted as a man in his thirties sauntered out of the living room. In the space of mere seconds, Alessandro had processed the guy and reached his verdict. This was no smarmy, overpaid young lawyer. This was a thug and, whatever was going on, Chase was afraid.

'And you are…?' If there was going to be a fight, then he was more than up for it.

'Not about to tell you, mate. Hang on…thought you said you'd broken up with lover boy? Lying to me, were you? Don't like lies…'

Alessandro clenched his fists. Chase had backed away

and was stammering out some sort of explanation which he barely registered. No, this wasn't going to do. He had hold of the man's tee-shirt and felt roughly one hundred and forty pounds of packed muscle try to squirm away from him. Escape was never destined to be. He propelled the man back towards the sitting room. Out of the corner of his eye, he could see that the room had been decimated. A black bin bag was stuffed to overflowing on the ground. Another was half-full. Was this the 'spot of bother' she was in?

'You're going to tell me what's going on…' He addressed her but kept his eye on his frantically writhing captive. The man was a bully; Alessandro could spot the signs a mile away. The sort of loser who didn't mind throwing his weight around with anyone weaker than him but would run a mile if faced with stiff competition. Alessandro prided himself on being stiff competition. He listened intently while Chase babbled something about Brian wanting money…taking her stuff…

The missing pieces were beginning to fall into place. So the money had been a legitimate request. She hadn't been trying to con gold out of him. 'Here's what you're going to do, buddy.' His voice was low, soft and razor-sharp. 'You're going to unload that bin bag and return all the nice lady's possessions to her. Then you're going to apologise and, when you've finished apologising, you're going to leave quietly through that front door and never show your face here again. Do you read me loud and clear?

'And just in case…' He tightened his stranglehold so that the man was gasping to catch his breath. 'You get it into your head that you can ignore what I'm telling you, here's what will happen to you if you do. I'll employ someone to dredge up every scrap of dirt on you—and I'm betting that there's a lot—and then I'm going to make sure that you get put behind bars and the key is conveniently thrown away. And don't think I won't do it. I will. And I'll enjoy every second of it.'

He watched in silence, arms folded, as his orders were obeyed. Out of the bin bag came all the bits and pieces which, Alessandro knew, would have taken Chase years to accumulate. Some were worthless, some—such as her computer, her tablet, the plasma-screen television which she had laughingly told him had been an absolute indulgence because she really didn't watch much TV—weren't.

His apology was grudgingly given until Alessandro ordered him to try harder, to say it like he meant it...

He left as quietly as he had been ordered to do. Then there was just the two of them, standing in a room that looked as though a bomb had exploded in it.

'I'm sorry,' Chase mumbled. Yet she was so glad that he had come because now she felt utterly safe. She moved to begin picking up some of her possessions from the ground, stacking them neatly on the sofa, very conscious of Alessandro's eyes on her. 'Why did you come?' she asked.

'You need something stiff to drink.'

'I'm fine.'

'Do you have any brandy?'

'I'm fine.' She finally met his eyes and hesitantly perched on the edge of the chair with her hands on her knees. 'There's half a bottle of wine in the fridge,' she offered when he continued to look at her in silence. 'It's all I can do by way of drink, I'm afraid. I don't keep spirits in the house.' Shock was creeping over her. She didn't want alcohol but she had to admit that she felt a little better after she had swallowed a mouthful from the glass he placed in her shaking hand a minute later.

'I guess you want to know what all that was about,' she said wearily.

'Understatement of the decade, Chase.'

Chase stared down at her fingers. She'd been rescued

by a man who had only returned to the scene to find out what was going on because he was like that—would never have been able to accept a brush off without demanding answers.

She would have to explain how it was that she knew Brian, how he had happened to be in her house. She would have to come clean about her background and know that he would be filled with contempt. Contempt for a woman who had lied about a fundamental aspect of her life and maintained the lie all through the time she had been seeing him. But there still remained a part of her that she refused to reveal, because to reveal it would be to lower herself even more in his estimation.

'You'd better sit down and I'll tell you. And then…' She took a deep breath and exhaled slowly. 'You can leave and it'll finally be over between us.'

CHAPTER NINE

SHE WAS STILL in her work clothes, the same dreary grey suit, except she looked...*rumpled.*

'Did he lay a finger on you?' Alessandro asked suddenly. 'Did he touch you?' This was as far out of his comfort zone as he had ever been. Even with parents intent on squandering their inheritance—parents who had been shining examples of irresponsibility; who had opened the doors of their various houses to artists and poets and playwrights, most of whom had been pleasantly stoned most of the time—through all that, he had never come into contact with the seedier side of life. The side of life that threw up people like the thug who had just been thrown off the premises. Even with diminishing wealth, he had still lived a sheltered, privileged life.

'No. No, he didn't.' Chase could see the incredulity stamped on his beautiful face. He was shocked at what he had found, shocked that the woman he thought came from a solid, middle-class background could know someone like Brian Shepherd. 'Although it's not unheard of for Brian to lay into someone just for the hell of it, never mind if he thinks they've done something to him.'

'How the hell do you know that guy, Chase?' Alessandro frowned. 'When you said that you couldn't tell me why you needed the money, did you mean that you owed that creep money?'

'No, I did *not* owe that creep any money. He just…' She stood up, suddenly restless, but then immediately sat back down because her legs felt like jelly.

'What, then…?'

'If you would just sit down and stop *prowling.*'

Alessandro paused to look at her narrowly. 'If you didn't owe the guy money, then why would he have gathered half of your possessions and stuffed them into a bin bag?' He sat on the chair facing her. Their body language was identical, both sitting forward, arms resting loosely on their thighs although, whilst Alessandro's expression was one of intense curiosity, Chase's was more resigned and reflective.

'Brian and Shaun were friends,' she said quietly, not daring to meet his eyes, fearful of what she would see there. 'They were friends from before I met Shaun, childhood friends, even though Brian was older. They grew up on the same council estate.'

'Which calls into question the type of man you chose to marry.'

'When you're young, it's very easy to get drawn in to the wrong crowd.'

'I'm trying to picture your parents allowing you to get drawn in to the wrong crowd. Or didn't they have any say in the matter? Maybe they were too busy projecting to happy times ahead in Australia…?'

'There *is* no Australia.'

'Sorry, but I'm not following you.'

Chase nervously tucked a strand of hair behind her ears. She wondered what hand of fate it was that had returned Alessandro to her life, only to have her fall in love with him all over again. Instead of getting him out of her system by sleeping with him, by putting that unfulfilled fantasy to rest, she had managed to well and truly cement him into every nook, cranny and corner of her being.

'My parents don't live in Australia. In fact, I have no parents. I was a foster-home kid. I was shuffled from family to family, never staying anywhere for very long. I never knew my father. My mother died when I was very little from a drugs overdose. I pretty much brought myself up. So, you see, everything you think you know about me is a lie.'

Of all the things Alessandro had been prepared for, this was not one of them. 'Lyla…?'

'Was the name I chose when I met you. When I thought that I could create…make myself out to be…'

'You fabricated everything.'

'No. Not everything!'

Alessandro slammed his hand on the side of his chair and vaulted to his feet. He felt tight in his skin. He needed to move. Energy was pouring through him and he was at a loss as to how to contain it. This must be what it felt like to imagine your feet were planted on solid ground only to discover that you were trying to balance on quicksand.

'Everything about you has been a lie from beginning to end. God. Why?'

'I made stuff up. I was young! I met you and I wanted to make a good impression.'

'Not only were you married, not only did you choose to conceal that fact from me eight years ago, but you also chose to conceal everything else. So your husband was… what, exactly? And how did you manage to make it to university? Or maybe you weren't a student at all. Were you? Or was that another lie?'

'Of course I was!' Chase cried, half-rising to her feet in an attempt to halt the flow of his scathing criticism. She sat back down as quickly as she had stood up. What else might she have hoped for? That he might have been understanding? Sympathetic? Why would he be? To him, she was now a confirmed liar and, if she had lied about everything, all those significant details, then what else might she have lied about? Her emotions? Her responses? It felt as though she had built a relationship on a house of cards and, now the cards were all toppling down, she had no idea how to start catching them before they all fell to the floor.

'Really? What strands am I supposed to start believing now?'

'I *was* a student at university,' she said with feverish urgency. 'I never did a lot of studying…' At this she laughed bitterly. Studying, when she was growing up, had not been seen as something worth wasting time doing. They had all known where they were destined to end up: out of work and on the dole, or else in no-hope jobs earning just enough to scrape by with a little moonlighting on the side.

'But I discovered that I barely needed to. I had a good memory. Brilliant, in fact. I would show up at school after a couple of days doing nothing, playing truant, and somehow I'd still be ahead of everyone in the class. I'd skim through a text book and manage to have instant recall of pretty much everything I'd read…'

The handful of teachers who had noticed that remarkable ability had been her salvation. Because of them she hadn't become a quitter, although she had learned to study undercover. There had never been any mileage in standing out.

She looked at him and held his inscrutable gaze. 'I guess you must find all of this completely alien. I don't suppose you've ever known anyone from the wrong side of the tracks…'

The chasm between them had never seemed wider, now that she was revealing the truth about her background. Even if she had been the person she had once claimed to be, the middle-class girl with the normal parents, there would still have been a chasm between them. Of course, he would have been attracted to her because of how she looked. Sadly, physical attributes were not destined to last; she accepted that, in an ideal world, he would have dumped her sooner or later anyway. He had been born into privilege, whatever his disruptive background, and he would always have ended up looking to settle with a woman from a similar background.

Not only had she lied to him, but she had lied to herself for ever thinking otherwise. And she had. When she had met him again and when she had fallen in love with him again. When she had nurtured silly dreams of 'what if?'s…

'Coming from the wrong side of the tracks is one thing,' Alessandro said brusquely. 'Lying about it is quite another. Were you ever going to tell me the truth?' His sense of betrayal overshadowed every other emotion, including anger.

'What would have been the point?' Chase asked defiantly. 'As you pointed out…as *we* agreed…it's not as though we were ever going anywhere with this relationship. Why would I have spoiled things with lots of truths I know you wouldn't have wanted to hear?'

Alessandro's jaw hardened. He took in her beautiful, stubborn face and had a very vivid image of the teenager she must have been: wild, drifting, incredibly bright, incredibly good-looking. 'Shaun…' Just uttering her ex-husband's name left a sour taste in his mouth. 'Must have thought he had won the lottery the day he met you—clever kid who could be his passport out of whatever dead-end life he was looking forward to leading.'

Chase looked up at him with some surprise. 'I never thought about it that way,' she said truthfully. 'I…' Was that how he had seen her, whilst making her believe that it had been the other way around? That *she* had been the lucky one to have been noticed by *him*? 'I met him when I was fifteen. He was the leader of the pack, so to speak. Everyone looked up to him even though he was younger than nearly all the guys in the gang. He was fed up living on the outskirts of Leeds. He said he wanted more. He said that London was the place to be.'

'And of course, he encouraged you to sign up to university life he knew that it was the best way out for him.'

'I don't know how I managed to get through all my exams, and I did them all a year ahead of everyone else,' Chase confessed. 'Maths, further maths, economics, geography…' But she had. Her teachers had seen to it that she'd sat them all. They were the ones who had insisted on university, who had filled in all the applications on her behalf while she had been busy having fun and running wild.

She had landed herself a place at one of the top universities in the country and had been amazed that she had accomplished such a feat. Only in retrospect had she appreciated the energy behind the scenes that had got her there.

'So you went to university and you got married.'

'The other way around, actually. I got married. Yes. And I went to university. I never expected to meet someone like you. Or anyone, for that matter.'

'And yet you did. And, instead of being truthful, you thought that it would be a much better idea to concoct a fairy-tale story about yourself.'

Chase heard the undercurrent of contempt mixed with bewilderment in his voice and inwardly winced. She was not the person she had pretended to be and that mattered to a man like him, a man who occupied a stratosphere of wealth and power that few could even dream about.

She wanted to shout at him that he didn't have a clue, that he couldn't possibly understand, but shouting wasn't going to do. Losing control wasn't going to do. She would offer him the explanation he deserved to hear with detachment and lack of passion. She would demonstrate that she was already breaking away from him, just as he was with her. She would leave with her dignity intact, as much as it could be. She would save her tears for later.

'Yes.' She tilted her chin up and steeled herself to meet his eyes squarely and without apology. 'I was young. I just…gave in to the temptation to turn myself into someone I wasn't. I made up the background I always wanted for myself.'

Alessandro felt another unwelcome, piercing tug of compassion at the thought that a middle-class background could have constituted her dream life. Most girls would have dreamt up stories of money, overseas holidays and parents with fast cars. She, on the other hand, had dreamt of what most other young girls of her age would have grumbled about and considered normal and boring.

He squashed any notion of compassion as fast as it raised its inappropriate head. The bottom line was that she was a compulsive liar, not to be trusted, never to be believed. He had come to get some truths out of her and he was getting them—in shed-loads.

'Which brings us to that piece of rubbish who was filling bin bags with your possessions.'

Getting to the heart of the matter and the reason he had shown up on her doorstep, Chase thought. Because, the faster he could wash his hands of her and clear off, the better.

'When we went to Italy, one of the girls who used to hang out in our gang was at the airport. I didn't see her.' But then, she hadn't had eyes for anyone but the man silently judging her now.

'She took pictures of us on her phone and posted them on a social networking site. Brian saw them, clocked the Louis Vuitton luggage and the chauffeur-driven car and decided that he would turn up on my doorstep and squeeze me for money. I don't know how he got my address, but there are so many ways of finding people; I don't suppose he had much trouble. He may just have gone to the place we were renting before Shaun died, got in touch with the landlord and got the forwarding address I gave him all those years ago. Who knows? He threatened to tell the people at work about my background… It would have spelled the end of my career. And he might have done a lot more besides…'

It seemed ironic now that the life she had built for herself could have been undone by something as crazy as someone taking a picture of her with Alessandro at an airport. There was no point dwelling on what was fair or what was unfair, she thought. The only way was to move forward. She kept her voice as modulated and toneless as she could.

'He was waiting for me when I got back to my house from Italy.'

Alessandro felt rage wash over him, a perfectly normal reaction to the thought of any thug lying in wait for a helpless victim.

'He told me that he wanted money and…that's when I asked you. I didn't want to, and if you *had* lent me the money I would have paid you back every penny.'

'You mean from the proceeds of the job you jacked in? Why did you do that?'

'I thought it best to resign just in case… I've never brought my past to my work. What would happen if Brian decided to show up at Fitzsimmons…?'

'Catastrophe—because they too were victims of your lies. They believed what you told them about your background, just like I did, didn't they?'

'I've never discussed my private life with anyone,' Chase mumbled, feeling even more of a hopeless liar, even though her lies had been through omission of the absolute truth. 'I've kept myself to myself. I fought hard to get where I was.'

'If you had told me the truth, I might have been inclined to give you the money.'

Chase shrugged. 'He would have come back for more. He knew where to find me. It was stupid of me to even… Well, in moments of panic we sometimes do stupid things.'

'He won't be back.'

'I know. And…and I'm very grateful to you for scaring him away. You probably threatened him with the one thing he would have taken notice of.' She wanted to smile, because who would have thought that a billionaire businessman from a cushy background could have had sufficient forcefulness to intimidate someone like Brian Shepherd into running scared? 'Look, I know you probably hate me for all of this…'

'You mean the fact that you were prepared to perpetuate a piece of fiction about yourself?' Alessandro strolled to stand in front of her, legs planted apart, hands at his sides.

Chase looked up at him reluctantly.

'What other pieces of fiction did you perpetuate?' he asked softly. 'No. There's just one more thing I need to get straight in my head.'

'What's—what's that?' she stammered uncertainly. She watched as he slowly leant over her and she half-closed her eyes as she inhaled his familiar scent. It rushed to her head like incense.

'This…' His mouth crushed her in a savage, punishing kiss and Chase helplessly yielded. She arched back in the chair, pulling him towards her, tasting him hungrily. She knew she shouldn't. She knew that it should be impossible to feel this driving, craven lust for a man who felt nothing but scorn towards her, but she couldn't seem to help herself.

There was a refrain playing at the back of her head that was telling her that this was the last time she would feel his lips on hers.

He pulled her to her feet and somehow they found themselves on the sofa, still entwined with one another. She was breathing heavily and she didn't stop him when he began undoing the buttons on her shirt, very soon losing patience. She heard the pop as a couple were ripped off. She wanted him so badly that she was shaking. Pride or no pride, she felt that she *needed* this final joining of their bodies. Her hands scrabbled to open his shirt so that she could feel the breadth of his chest and she moaned when, eventually, her fingers were splayed against it.

Her nipples tingled against her lacy bra. He cupped her breast with his hand and then pushed it underneath the bra, shoving the bra up so that he could suck on her nipple, drawing the stem into his mouth and swirling his tongue against it until she was half-crying for more.

As he suckled, he nudged her legs apart and then his hand was there, not even bothering to pull down her undies but delving underneath them, finding her wetness and exploring every inch of it with his fingers.

He still hadn't taken off a stitch of his own clothes. She had managed to undo a few buttons on his shirt and had yanked it out from the waistband of his trousers. She feverishly tried to complete the task of undressing him but he wasn't helping. She couldn't get to the zip of his trousers, although she could feel the bulge of his erection.

She gave up as he continued driving his fingers against her, pausing in the rhythmic movement only to insert them into her, into that place where she knew she wanted his rock-hard shaft to be instead.

He reared up and yanked down his trousers and, with his hand tangled in her hair, he guided her to his erection and stifled a groan when she took him into her mouth.

Through half-opened eyes, he watched as she sucked and licked him. She knew just how to rouse him down there with her hands and her mouth and he let her.

She might be a liar; he might not be able to trust her as far as he could throw her—because who could ever trust a woman who made a habit of fabricating her life story?—but she certainly knew just which buttons to press.

He tugged her away from him and sank onto her. Her breasts, with the bra pushed up above them, were full and ripe and irresistible. With a groan of satisfaction, he covered them with his mouth, until the pouting buds were wet and hard and he continued, giving her no respite, until she was wriggling like an eel, desperate for more.

Her hair was all over the place and her cheeks were flushed, her mouth slightly parted, showing her perfect, pearly-white teeth. She had sunbathed in the nude by the pool in Italy, and her body was a perfect honey colour.

How well he knew this body. How much of it he had explored and committed to memory, from the freckle by her nipple to the tiny mole on her upper arm.

He pulled down her panties, flattened his hand between her legs and then stroked her down there, harder and faster, until he could feel her orgasm building beneath his fingers. He didn't stop and when she came he watched: watched her eyes flutter; watched her breathing catch in her throat for a few seconds; watched her whole body arch, stiffen and finally slacken as the waves of pleasure finally subsided, leaving her limp.

'Alessandro…' She reached for him and he stayed her hand, circling her wrist before releasing her and standing up.

For a few seconds, Chase was completely bewildered. When he began to zip up his trousers, she clambered into a sitting position and looked at him speechlessly.

'What are you doing?'

'What does it look like I'm doing?'

'We were making love.'

'I was proving to myself that the way you responded to me wasn't yet another lie.'

'How could you say that?' She itched to pull him back

to her but he was already turning away, doing up his buttons and taking his time, as cool as a cucumber. 'I never, *never,* pretended with you. Not about that…'

Alessandro steeled himself. She had made him cry once. The memory of that rose uninvited like poison from the deepest recesses of his mind. He had given a lot to her and her betrayal then had rocked his foundations. Never again.

'So it would seem.' He turned around to look at her. She was utterly dishevelled and utterly bewitching. 'I came here to get answers from you and I got them, Chase. Now the time has come for me to tell you goodbye. It's been… I would say fun, but what I'd really mean is…it's been a learning curve. You can congratulate yourself on teaching me the dangers of taking people at face value.'

'Alessandro!'

'What?' In the process of heading for the door, he half-turned towards her. His eyes were flat, hard and cold. There was a tense silence that stretched between them to breaking point.

Chase found that she didn't know what to say. She just didn't want him to go. Not just yet. Her body was still burning from where he had touched her, where he had deliberately touched her, turning her on, bringing her to a shuddering orgasm just to prove to himself that the attraction she'd claimed to feel for him was real. It was humiliating, yet she still couldn't bear the thought of him walking away. How on earth had she let it go this far? How was it that the control she had spent eight years building, the ability to arrange her life just how she wanted it without reference to anyone else, had been washed away by a man who had always been unsuitable and inappropriate?

'Nothing.'

He looked at her for a few seconds, shrugged and then he was gone. Just like that.

Chase was left staring at the empty doorway. He was

gone and he would never be coming back. She disgusted him. Her awful life, her sleazy ex-friends…

And he'd had the nerve to look contemptuous because once upon a time she had given in to the temptation to make it all go away by pretending to be somebody else! She might not have known about his wealth back then, but she had known with some unerring sixth sense that he would not be the kind of guy who would find any woman who came from her background attractive or in any way suitable.

And of course, she *hadn't* been suitable. She had been married, for starters. But she had seized that window of forbidden, youthful pleasure and now, all this time later, she was paying heavily for it.

She spent two hours returning all the stuff Brian had hauled off shelves and from drawers back to their rightful places. She washed a lot of it. The thought of his hands on her things made her shudder with distaste.

She hoped that by occupying herself she might take her mind off Alessandro but, all the while, he was in her head as she remembered the things they had done together, the conversations they had had.

She shakily told herself that it was a good thing that they were finished. It had been destined to end and the sooner the better. How much worse would she have felt had they ended it in two months' time? Two months during which she would have just continued falling deeper and deeper in love with him! The longer they lasted, the more difficult it would have been to unpick and disentangle her chaotic emotions. She should be thankful!

And yet, thankful was the very last thing she felt. She felt devastated, tearful and…*ashamed.*

More than anything else, she was angry with him for making her feel that way. She was angry with him for being hard line; for not having an ounce of sympathy in him; for not even trying to see her point of view. She had known from the outset that his sole motivation for sleeping with her was to exact some sort of revenge, to have that wheel turn full circle, to take what he thought had been promised to him eight years ago. Yet, hadn't he got to know her *at all* during that period? Had she just been his lover and *nothing more*?

They hadn't been rolling around on a mattress all of the time. There had been so many instances when they had talked, when the past hadn't existed, just the present, just two people getting to know one another. Or so it had felt to her.

She hated him for wiping that all away as though none of it had existed. She hated him for finding it so easy to write her off as though she was worthless.

Over the next week, as she came closer and closer to her final day at Fitzsimmons, the frustration and anger continued to build inside her. If only she could have maintained the anger, she might have felt protected, but there were so many chinks through which she recalled small acts of thoughtfulness, his wonderful wit, his sharp intellect, his lazy, sexy smile. What they had had all those years ago had been unbearably intense and that intensity had given the times they had shared recently a deep level of communication that was almost intuitive. She missed that. She missed him.

She hadn't heard a word from him. He had truly disappeared from her life—although, by all accounts, he had been on the scene far more than anticipated at the shelter, where, from what Beth had blithely told her, he appeared suddenly to have taken a keen interest in all the renovations she had planned.

'He has so many good suggestions for how the money could be spent!' Beth had enthusiastically listed all the suggestions while Chase had listened in resentful silence. 'He's also been kind enough to put us in touch with contacts he has in the contracting business so that we can get the best possible deal!' Chase had muttered something under her breath which she hoped didn't sound like the unladylike oath it most certainly was.

Beth had no idea of the history she and Alessandro had shared. It would have been petty and small-minded not to have responded with a similar level of enthusiasm to the hard-nosed billionaire businessman who had previously threatened a hostile buy-out, only to morph into a saint with a positively never-ending supply of 'brilliant ideas' and 'amazingly useful contacts'.

On the Friday, exactly a week after he had walked out of her house, there was a little leaving drinks party for her at the office, to which far more people turned up than she had expected, bearing in mind she had not been the most sociable of the team out of work.

She would be sorely missed, her boss said in the little speech he gave to the assembled members of staff. Everyone raised their glasses of champagne. These were the people she had kept at arm's length, burying herself in her work and always feeling the unspoken differences between them. And yet, as various of her colleagues came over to talk to her, she could tell that they were genuinely delighted that she intended to pursue her pro bono work in a firm that was solely dedicated to doing that.

Numbers and email addresses were exchanged with various girls whom she had known on a purely superficial basis.

When she tentatively volunteered the information that she would find it tough financially because she had no family to help her out if she started going under, there were no gasps of horror. When she confessed to a couple of the girls that she loved pro bono work because, growing up on a council estate, she had seen misery first-hand and had always wanted to do something about it, they hadn't walked away, smirking. They had been interested.

By the end of the evening, she had drunk more than she had intended but had also made friends in unexpected places.

Had she made a mistake in erecting so many protective defence mechanisms around her that she had failed to let anyone in? Had her cool distance been a liability in the end, rather than an asset? Had her detachment, which had been put in place for all the right reasons, become a habit which had imprisoned her more firmly than the solid steel bars of a prison cell?

Her thoughts were muddled and all over the place when, at a little after nine, she hailed a black cab to take her back to her house. When she closed her eyes and rested her head back on the seat, she could see Alessandro, a vibrant image hovering in the deepest recesses of her mind.

She had told him bits and pieces of the truth. Was that sufficient? An enormous sense of lassitude washed over her when she thought about the rest of what had been left unsaid.

So, nothing would change. He would still despise her. He would still be repelled by the person he thought she had turned out to be, but wouldn't she feel better in herself? Wouldn't coming clean, laying all her cards on the table, leave her with a clear conscience when she walked away? And wouldn't a clear conscience be a far better companion when she lay down in her bed at night and allowed thoughts of him to proliferate in her head?

She had given away more of herself today with her colleagues than she had in all the years she had worked alongside them, and it had felt good.

She leant forward, told the cab driver to turn around and gave him Alessandro's address.

She had no idea whether he would be in or not. It was a Friday night and face it, he was once again a free, single and eligible guy who might very well have jumped back on the sexual merry-go-round.

The alcohol had given her Dutch courage. Even as the taxi pulled up outside his magnificent house, her nerves didn't start going into automatic meltdown. She had reached a point of realising that she had nothing left to lose.

Her hand only shook a little as she reached for the doorbell and pressed hard, the very same way he had pressed *her* doorbell when he had walked in on Brian depleting her house of all its worldly goods.

On his third whisky, Alessandro heard the distant peal of his doorbell and debated whether he should bother getting it or not. A package was due to be delivered by courier. Work related. Could he really be bothered?

His torpor exasperated him but it had dogged his every waking moment ever since he had walked out of her house. Try as he might, he hadn't been able to shake it. The confines of his opulent office had felt restricting. He had found himself avoiding it, not caring what his secretary thought, going to the shelter practically every day.

It was Friday night and, whilst his head told him that it was time to get back on the horse, to find a replacement for the woman with whom he should never have become entangled all over again, his feet had brought him right back to his house and towards the drinks cabinet. A bracing evening diet of whisky and soda had felt eminently more tempting than shallow conversation with the airheads and bimbos who would circle him at the slightest given opportunity.

Of course, there was a limit to how long this crazy state of affairs could continue. Swearing softly under his breath, and with the glass of whisky still in his hand, he strolled to the front door and pulled it open. On his lips were a few select curses for whatever imbecile of a courier had had the temerity to keep his finger on the buzzer when he, Alessandro, was in the process of working his way down to the bottom of his glass, through which he hoped to see the world as an altogether rosier place.

'Alessandro. You're…' Any hint of incipient nerves flew through the window at the sight of an Alessandro who, for the first time ever, did not seem to be completely in control of all his faculties. 'Are you *drunk*?'

Alessandro leaned against the doorframe and swallowed back the remnants of whisky in his glass. 'What are you doing here at this hour? It's after nine. And I'm not drunk.'

The woman he had walked away from. He tried to think of all the pejorative adjectives that had sprung so easily to mind when he had last seen her. Before he had endured the most hellish week of his entire life. Where the hell had his bullish confidence gone about the fact that she was not worth his while? And where had she been anyway? He checked his watch and saw that it was actually a little before ten. Had she been out *partying*? A tidal wave of jealousy left him shaken.

'Living it up, Chase?' His mouth twisted as he focused on the much less prim and proper attire she was wearing, a fitted burgundy dress rather than her uniform of suits which was all he had ever seen her in for work.

'I know you're probably surprised to see me here. Shocked, even.' Although there was a glass in his hand and it was empty. Had he company? A woman? Chase refused to let that thought take shape and gain momentum.

Alessandro noticed that she had neatly avoided answering his question. He shouldn't even care. In fact, hadn't he made his mind up that he wanted nothing further to do with her? That he could never trust a woman who had lied to him? Hadn't he? 'What are you doing here? Thought you might pay a little social call? On your way back from wherever you've been out partying?'

So his mood hadn't changed. He was still hostile and contemptuous, still ready to attack. 'I haven't been *out partying*, Alessandro. I… It was my last day at work today. There was champagne at the office, that's all. I…I've come because there are some things I still need to say to you.'

So she had just been cooped up at the office. He felt some of his dark mood evaporate. She had more to say to him? Well, why not? The choice was either that or the rest of the whisky to keep him company. He turned on his heels, leaving the door open and Chase, after a few seconds' hesitation, followed him into the house.

CHAPTER TEN

SHE FOLLOWED HIM into the sitting room and immediately spotted the bottle of whisky, which was half-empty.

'How much of this stuff have you *drunk*?' she gasped in amazement.

'I think it's safe to say that my drinking habits are none of your business.' The burgundy dress lovingly clung to her body and outlined curves in all the right places. He could feel himself getting turned on and he scowled because the last thing he needed was his wilful body doing its own thing. He subsided on the sofa, legs apart, his body language aggressively, defensively masculine.

'So, what are you here for?' he demanded, following her with a glowering expression as she hesitated by the door. He watched broodingly as she took a deep breath and walked to one of the pale-cream leather chairs by the fireplace, a modern built-into-the-wall affair which she had variously claimed to have both loved and detested.

'I didn't ask,' Chase said in a thin voice. 'But is someone here with you?'

'Is someone here with me? Does it look like I have company?' He gestured to the empty room.

'You're drinking, Alessandro…' She nodded to the whisky bottle which bore witness to her statement. 'And since when do you drink on your own? Especially spirits. Didn't you once tell me that drinking spirits on your own was a sign of an alcoholic in the making? Didn't you tell me that your parents put you off giving in to vices like that in a big way? That they were a bigger warning against drinking, smoking and taking drugs than any lecture anyone could have given you?'

Alessandro's expression darkened. 'And since when are you my guilty conscience?' he demanded belligerently. He couldn't take his eyes off her. It felt as though he hadn't seen her in a hundred years and, whilst he knew that that certainly wasn't a healthy situation given the fact that she had been dispatched from his life, he still couldn't help himself, and that helplessness made him feel even more of a sad loser.

'I'm not.' Chase stared down at her entwined fingers in silence for a couple of seconds. Now that she was here, sitting in front of him, the nerves which had been absent on her trip over were gathering pace inside her. She had come to tell him how she felt but her moment of bravery was in danger of passing. She wasn't his guilty conscience. She was nothing to him. She was surprised that he hadn't slammed the door in her face, and she took some courage from the fact that he hadn't.

'I've…I've…managed to get a couple of leads on some promising jobs,' she heard herself saying, a propos nothing in particular. 'Out of London. One in Manchester. The other in Surrey. I guess I'll sell my place and move sticks. It'll be cheaper, anyway. I would probably be able to afford something bigger.'

'And you've come here to tell me this because…?'

'I haven't come here to tell you that. I just thought… Well…'

'Get to the point, Chase.' When he thought of her leaving London, he felt as though a band of pure ice had wrapped itself around his heart like the tenacious tendrils of creeping ivy.

She sprang to her feet and began walking restively around the room. It was a big room. The colours were pale and muted, from the colour of the walls to the soft leather furniture. It was modern and, when she had first seen it, she hadn't, been able to decide whether she liked it or not. Certainly, right at this very moment, it chilled her to the bone, but then wasn't that just her fear and trepidation taking its toll? The hard contours of his face spoke volumes for his lack of welcome. He might not have slammed the door in her face but he clearly didn't want her in his house. She felt that little thread of courage begin to seep slowly away.

'Do you remember that…that day, Alessandro?'

'Be specific. What day in particular are you talking about? The day you lied about the fact that you were a happily married woman, or the day you lied about the fact that the loving parents in Australia were a work of fiction…?'

Chase fought against the sneering coolness in his voice and sat back down, this time on the sofa with him, but at the furthest end of it.

'We met at that pub. Do you remember? The one by the park?'

He remembered. He could even remember what she had been wearing. It came to him with such vivid clarity that he almost thought that it had been lying in wait for eight years, just at the edges of his memory: a pair of very faded jeans, some plimsolls which had once been white but were scuffed way past their original colour and a light-blue jumper, the sleeves of which were long enough for her to tuck her hands inside them. Which she had done as she had delivered her blow.

'I told you about Shaun.'

'Believe me, I haven't forgotten that special moment in my life.'

'Please don't be sarcastic, Alessandro. This is really

hard for me. I just want you to listen, because you were right when you said that we had unfinished business between us. We did. And, for me at least, we still have until you hear me out. Or, rather, *I* still do….'

The palms of her hands felt sweaty and she smoothed them over the burgundy dress. 'Eight years ago, I fell in love with you.' She braved his silent stare and willed herself to continue. 'I was married and, believe me, I shouldn't have looked at you, far less spoken to you, but I did. You have no idea what you did for me. Being with you was like being free for the first time in my life. I finally understood what all those silly romance novels were all about.'

Alessandro frowned. This was hardly the direction he'd expected the conversation to go in. 'If you're hoping to pull on my heart strings, then you're barking up the wrong tree. I have perfect recall of your little speech to me. It involved you telling me that Shaun was the great love of your life, that it had been fun seeing me, but you were only in it for some help with work…hoped I didn't get the wrong idea. I'm recalling the moment you waved your wedding ring in my face and pulled out a photo of your loved one.'

'Yes.'

'So where are you going with this, exactly? Why have you come here to waste my time?' Another shot of whisky would have gone down a treat but he *did* remember what he had said to her about his parents teaching him the horrors of having no control, by example.

'I was an idiot when I married Shaun…' Chase stared absently into the distance. 'I was incredibly young and it seemed like an exciting thing to do. Or…or maybe not, thinking about it now. *Shaun* told me it would be an exciting thing to do and I went along with it because I had already figured out that it didn't pay to disagree with anything he said.'

'Watch out. You're in danger of wiping some of the shine from your blissfully joyous married life.'

'There was never any shine on it, and I wasn't blissfully married,' Chase told him abruptly. She refocused on his face to find him watching her carefully. When she thought about the horror that had been her married life with Shaun, she wanted to cry for those wasted years, but the self-control she had built up over the years stood her in good stead.

Alessandro found that he was holding his breath. 'Another lie, Chase?' But he wanted to hear what she had to say even though he told himself that he wasn't going to fall for anything she told him. Once bitten, twice shy.

'I haven't come here to try and make you believe me, Alessandro,' Chase said with quiet sincerity. 'I know you probably won't anyway. I know I've lied to you in the past and you'll never forgive me. You've made that crystal-clear. I'm here because I *need* to tell you everything. And, when I'm finished, I'll walk out that door and you'll never see me again.

'When I met you for the first time, I began something that was dangerous, although you weren't to know that. I've thought about what you said, about Shaun hitching his wagon to me because he knew that he would be able to go further with me shackled to his side. I think you were right, although at the time I didn't see it that way. By the time I made it to university, I'd lost the ability to think independently. My studies were the only thing keeping me going. We'd come to London and I had been taken away from my friends, from everything I knew, although I guess you would find "everything I knew" hardly worth knowing anyway. Shaun was in his element. I was married to him and he was in complete control, and he enjoyed making sure he exercised that control.'

'What are you telling me?'

'I'm telling you that I was an abused wife. The sort of pathetic woman you would find contemptible. The sort of woman who can really understand how all those women at Beth's shelter feel. Why do you imagine I have such empathy for them?'

'When you say abused…?'

'Physically, mentally, emotionally. Shaun was never fussy when it came to laying down laws. He used whatever methods suited him at the time.' She tilted her chin defiantly. She had come to say her piece and he could save his contempt for after she'd left. That was what her expression was telling him.

'He was very clever when it came to making sure he hurt me in ways that weren't visible. He let me out of his sight to attend lectures and tutorials but I was under orders to return home immediately, not to hang around and certainly never to cultivate any sort of friendship with any of the other students. I was just glad to be out of his presence. Anything was better than nothing and, besides, I thrived on the academic work. I found it all ridiculously easy.

'One of the first things I'm going to do when I leave London is to find the teachers who encouraged me and tell them how valuable their input was.' She made sure that he got the message that she wasn't looking for anything from him, that she was moving on, that she had her independence, whatever her story was.

'You say you were…in love with me. Why didn't you leave him?' *Because,* Alessandro thought, *I was certainly head over heels in love with you. I would have protected you.*

It was the first time he had ever really and truly given that notion house room and, now that he had, everything seemed to fall neatly into place. The manner in which she had departed from his life had altered his view of women and had, more profoundly, altered the sort of women he went out with. He had developed a healthy mistrust of anything that remotely smelled of commitment and had programmed every single relationship he'd had to fail by systematically dating women in whom he was destined to lose interest after very short periods of time. In the wake of losing his heart to a woman who had deceived him, he had simply pressed the self-destruct button inside him.

And then she had returned to his life under extraordinary circumstances. He had held her to ransom and told himself that he was exacting revenge. In fact, he had told himself a lot of things. The one single thing he had failed to tell himself—because he could see now that he just couldn't have brought himself to even think it—was that he still wanted her because, quite simply, he was still in love with her.

Chase sensed the infinitesimal shift in him. Was it too much to ask that he at least believed her?

'I couldn't,' she said, flushing. 'I've become very independent over the years. It's been so important for me to stand on my own two feet, to give nothing of myself to anyone, to make sure that no one had control over me. But back then there was no way that I had the inner strength to try and escape. He had sapped me of all my confidence. Anyway…'

She stared down at her fingers, drained from the confidences she was giving away. 'I haven't come here to make excuses, just to tell you things as they were. I met you and it was wonderful but Shaun found out. He got hold of my mobile phone; I had been stupid enough to have one of your text messages there. I had forgotten to delete it. It was arranging to meet for lunch. He went crazy. I can't tell you, but I was terrified for my life. He threatened to kill us both if I didn't end it and, to make sure I did what he said, he made me arrange the location we were supposed to meet. He told me exactly what I was to say to you, and he was sitting at the table behind us the whole time I gave you that little speech about being a happily married woman…'

'My God.'

'I could never have told you about how things really were and I still didn't want to when I saw you again because I was…ashamed. I knew how you'd react. I knew all your opinions of me as a strong career woman with a mind of her own would evaporate and I would be just a pathetic, abused woman, like all those women you didn't give a hoot about when you were going to buy the shelter and have them dispossessed.' She took a deep breath and made eye contact with him but what she saw there was far from contempt. The silence stretched between them until it was at breaking point.

'If we had met later…' she said in a low voice, half-talking to herself '…then things might have been different. Even if I'd still been with Shaun, I would have had more self-confidence. I would have had my degree, a good job; I would have had the courage to walk away from him, but at that point in my life it just wasn't there.'

'And then,' Alessandro said heavily, 'we met again and I hardly inspired the trust you needed to open up. I blackmailed you into sleeping with me…'

'I *wanted* to sleep with you,' Chase confirmed in a driven voice. 'I would never have let myself be blackmailed into doing anything. I said so at the time and I meant it. I'd learnt the hard way not to let anyone else have control over me. I *wanted* to sleep with you and I don't regret it.'

'And what happened to the…love?' Alessandro asked so quietly that she had to strain to hear him.

'I still love you, Alessandro,' she said proudly. 'And I don't regret that either. So, there you are.' She stood up and brushed her skirt to distract herself from speculating on what was going on in his head.

'Not so fast!'

Chase looked up at him in surprise. His command was imperious but there was a hesitancy underlying it that wormed its way past her common sense.

'I'm glad you came,' he said, flushing darkly and looking so suddenly vulnerable that she wanted to sidle a little closer to him, just to make sure that her eyes weren't playing tricks on her. She remained where she was, resisting the impulse. 'I'm glad you were honest with me. Yes, when we met again…'

Alessandro raked his fingers through his hair and shook his head with a rueful smile that did even more disastrous things to her common sense. 'It all came rushing back at me. I hadn't realised how much I remembered and I certainly didn't get why it was that I remembered so well. I just knew that I still…wanted you. Somewhere along the line, I figured out that I had never stopped wanting you. I couldn't make sense of it, couldn't understand how I could still want a woman who I felt had betrayed me in the worst possible way. Don't get me wrong; I understand why you wanted to keep your secrets to yourself, why you felt that they would be too dark for me to handle, but if only I had known…'

'Nothing would have changed, Alessandro. Nothing has changed now.'

'No, nothing's changed and everything's changed. You're the same person you always were, Chase, whatever you went through. What you mean to me will always be the same, just as it was all those years ago. You will always be the girl I fell in love with but was too damned stupid to own up to. I let pride rule my behaviour and only now… Well, I'm still in love with you.'

Chase wondered whether she had heard correctly or whether wishful thinking had taken complete control. Was it even possible to hear something you wanted to hear because you wanted it *so badly*? She found that she was holding her breath.

'Um…did you just say… Did you just tell me…?'

'That I'm in love with you? Yes, I did. And I'll tell you again if you'd move a little closer so that I don't have to shout across the width of the sofa.'

'It's not a big sofa,' Chase said faintly.

'Right now, with you sitting at the other end of it, it feels as wide as a canyon.'

She shuffled along and slipped into his arms with a soaring feeling of utter elation. 'What if I hadn't come tonight?'

'I would never have let you go. The past week has been the worst of my life. I've never hated my office more. I lost interest in deals, going to meetings, reading emails… I know more now about that shelter than I would ever have thought possible.'

'Beth said you'd been a frequent visitor.' She curled into him and heard the beating of his heart.

'It made me feel close to you,' he confessed shakily, 'Although I never faced up to that. I love you, Chase. I love you for the person you are now and I loved you for the person you were then. I can't live without you. I want you to be my wife. Will you marry me? Within the next hour?'

Chase lifted her head and laughed, her eyes glowing with happiness. 'Within the next hour might be stretching it,' she said softly. 'But, yes, I'll be your wife.'

'And never leave my side?'

'You're stuck with me for ever…' And never had the thought of being stuck with someone for ever sounded so good.

* * * * *